Man's Natural Predator

by

Phil J. Briggs

authorHOUSE®

AuthorHouse™ UK Ltd.
500 Avebury Boulevard
Central Milton Keynes, MK9 2BE
www.authorhouse.co.uk
Phone: 08001974150

©2009 Phil J. Briggs. All rights reserved.

No part of this book may be reproduced, stored in a retrieval system, or transmitted by any means without the written permission of the author.
ISBN: 978-1-4389-2541-7 (sc)
First published by AuthorHouse 4/29/2009

ISBN: 978-1-4389-2541-7

This book is printed on acid-free paper.

Man's Natural Predator

Phil J. Briggs

Chapter One

Looking at the paperwork Richard, a Customs & Excise officer of Portsmouth dock, checked the lot number to ensure it matched the container that somehow had been over looked and appeared to have been in quarantine for over 50 years. He scratched the back of his neck and exhaled slightly as he moved forward towards the container. Slowly raising the heavy bolt croppers he was holding till level with the security tag, which held the industrial lock in place, he positioned the jaws either side of the lock tab. Slowly closing the jaws grip, he flexed his overweight body to summon the strength to cut the tab clean in two. Almost in slow motion the two sun faded halves of the tab gently fell to the floor, as they settled, a chilling wind picked up and spun them round in a circular motion lifting them several inches off the ground.

As quickly as the wind had picked up, it dropped, releasing its prisoners, which fell to the floor like a couple of dead stones. Richard a little disturbed by this took a cautious step back from the container and looked it up and down with an inner feeling that something was not quite right.

The unusually sunny day for mid April suddenly faded, as thick black clouds formed, creating a stormy dark almost night like environment. Keeping his eyes fixed on the container, Richard fumbled around his feet to locate the disc cutter which he needed to remove the lock. Finding the handle he swiftly picked up the disc cutter jerking it to establish a good hold on the handle. With the other hand he located the pull cord to start the petrol driven beast. Pulling the cord in a clean upward motion, the disc cutter sprung into life and emitted a small black puff of smoke before levelling at a steady idle. Squeezing and releasing the trigger the chainsaw responded Vroom, vroom. Releasing the trigger Richard took a second to look up at the sky, assessing if it was going to pour down.

Muttering to himself, "Fucking British weather should have moved to Oz when I had the chance to."

A broken clap of thunder rolled, which made Richard look a little longer as he did not recall seeing any signs of lightning. Not particularly concerned by the strange change in weather he revved the disc cutter once more and advanced towards the container. Gritting his teeth Richard lifted the heavy machine up to the lock and embedded the disc in the bolt of the lock. As the disc engaged the rounded tough surface of the bolt it skipped briefly before taking its first deep bite. Locking his body Richard pressed harder to keep the disc cut straight and clean, increasing the pressure on the trigger the disc cutter easily cut through the 20mm bolt. Lowering the disc cutter and releasing the trigger Richard put it on the floor and pressed the kill switch.

Taking the paperwork out of his top pocket Richard again examined the detail to understand what should be in the container, scanning the form he was surprised to read 'Personal Artefacts'

Placing the paperwork back in his top pocket, Richard used both hands to grasp the handle which would open the giant mystery steel box. Widening his stance, he knew that the mechanism would be hard to move as it had been unopened for many years. Using all of his strength and body weight Richard forced the handle upwards allowing the handle to rise over its locking plates. Turning the handle through its operating range the multi dead lock bolts of the container dropped into the open position. Richard took a deep breath and opened the first heavy steel door swinging it to his right side freeing the second door to be opened. Grabbing the second door and aggressively opening it, Richards jaw dropped open and a dumb like expression covered his face as the contents were revealed.

Surrounding the decorative coffin were several large old looking wooden chests. Richard surprised with his find, edged slowly into the container very unsure of what was before him. A slight white mist appeared to be settling on the floor and gently flowed towards the open doors, hugging the contours of whatever it passed over and finally escaping into Portsmouth's atmosphere. Richard looked around the container calmly, searching for a chiller unit and wondered if the container was refrigerated. Shrugging his shoulders he dismissed this thought and took another timid step forward. As the mist cleared Richard took a mental note of how many chests surrounded the coffin, gently nodding his head as he acknowledged each one.

"Four, five, six, seven," he muttered as he removed the paperwork from his top pocket.

Looking over the detail of the itinerary of the T1 form he noticed the detail only expressed eight boxes. Knowing that the insufficient detail on the form and that the shipment had come from Romania, which kind of explained why the container was being held. Slightly less anxious Richard turned and boldly walked back out of the container to his tool chest. Opening the bottom draw he removed his crow bar and trusty club hammer, which gave him a pleasant feeling of security.

Returning into the container he targeted the nearest chest, which appeared similar to that found on a pirate ship, a rich dark oak wood with black steel plated fastening brackets. Ramming the end of his crow bar into a vulnerable area surrounding the lock, Richard found himself smiling in a boyish manner and thinking,

'I have found treasure.'

As the lock separated from the chest and fell to the floor, Richard gently pushed his glasses up the bridge of his nose to ensure his vision would be clear. He paused for a moment and then thrust his hand in his side pocket of his combat type trousers, pulling out a pair of surgical gloves. Inserting his right hand into one glove and then quickly followed by the left hand, Richard knelt down and lowered his head to gain the first sneaky peak of the content of the chest, expecting to find gold coins, jewels and precious stones, he startled himself and dropped the lid when he saw a neatly organised set of vials, which all appeared to be filled with blood.

"What the?" he said under his breath knowing that the legislation even 50 years ago to transport blood was very strict, suddenly it all did not make sense.

Now baffled and curious Richard raced to the next chest madly striking the crow bar into it. Taking large chunks of wood from the chest the lock soon was free and fell to the floor. Throwing the lid open his forehead raised as he saw more neatly organised blood. Repeating this on chests three and four the find was the same, opening chest five Richard suddenly felt quite cold and experienced a momentary paralysing sensation as he viewed the floor of the chest laden with empty vials. Quickly looking at the coffin and then again at the empty vials Richard thought,

'Shit, bloody Dracula is probably in there'.

He rushed over to the sixth chest and cracked it open. To his surprise he found the content to be what he had expected when opening the first one, wads of bound U.S. dollars, which when put in the chest were more than likely new. Looking at the band round the notes expressing $10,000 Richard took a second to work out there must be in excess of $500,000 dollars in the chest, which briefly distracted him from his previous thought of vampires. Opening the final chest Richard found this was also full of unused dollars and couldn't help thinking,

'With the current exchange rates, I bet who ever owns this money didn't expect it to be worth half of what it was when it set sail'.

Chuckling to himself he remembered the fact that there was a very elaborate coffin just three feet from him and an old fashion blood bank, which soon refocused his thoughts to what was in the coffin.

Checking his mobile for signal he pondered for a moment,
'Come on you silly old sod, you don't believe in that mumbo jumbo stuff. What an excellent way to cover up a drug stash make it look a bit spooky, that's why it is probably been sat here for such a long time. I bet I will find half a tonne of cocaine in there, not some blood sucking dude all dressed in black.'
Taking his time to collate his thoughts he realised his hands were actually shaking as he once again glanced at his mobile.
'I suppose I should really call the drug squad in and let them deal with it, but what if there are no drugs how stupid will I look? If there is I will be famed as finding one of Britain's biggest hauls single handily. Come on pull yourself together man, you're 48 years of age there are no such things as vampires.'
Richard realised that his mouth had gone very dry and gulped hard to swallow, looking over his left shoulder his face squinted as he decided he was going to open the coffin. Gently tapping the crow bar in his left palm, he nervously moved towards the centre of the coffin. Taking the bar in two hands Richard scanned the lid line to establish the best place to inset the metal claw. Recognising what appeared as a slight default in the seal, he confidently rammed the claw with accuracy into this exact spot. Securing a good bite he levered the bar

downwards, as his entire body weight was upon the bar he did not see that the claw was losing its grip, suddenly the claw popped out.

"Ahhhh!" he screamed as he found he could not recover from his over balanced position and fell to the ground. The loud metallic sound of the crow bar hitting the container floor seemed amplified and echoed for several seconds drowning out Richards cry. Shaking his head Richard slowly got back to his feet and looked at the coffin,

'You're not getting the better of me' when a loud repeated bang broke his thoughts and made him leap several feet backwards from the coffin.

"Hahhah Hahhahh, you should have seen your face!" Tony roared with laughter.

Tony a colleague of Richard, found it quite funny to play practical jokes and lowered himself and rested both hands on his knees as his laughter became accompanied by tears,

"Oh man, you shit a brick big time!"

"Nice one Tony, I think you are right. I think I have just crapped in my pants, you bloody dickhead."

Tony had not taken the time to actually look around the inside of the container and asked,

"What the fuck is going on in here, you into some weird shit, you want to talk about?" as he looked around at the contents.

"Tony, give me a hand over here, got to get the lid off this to see what is being stowed."

"On your bike, you must need your nut checking," Tony replied.

"Come on you big tart, not scared of Ghosts are you?"

"Don't be daft but shouldn't we get the drug squad involved?"

"Come on its nearly open,"

Tony not convinced this was the right way forward, dragged his feet and made his way towards Richard. As he walked towards Richard he looked at his watch and said, "Ricky old boy, its ten minutes until I clock out, can we not do this tomorrow?"

"That's the trouble with you youngsters nowadays, no loyalty whatsoever!"

Tony, a fit man in his late twenties, was thinking ahead as he was meeting a buddy soon after his shift finished,

"Yeah yeah, Pappa Smurf. Let's get on with it then, haven't got all day." Tony muttered.

With the crow bar firmly in position, both Richard & Tony applied a strong and constant force to the bar. The bar flexed slightly before the lid of the coffin lifted briefly in each corner before settling again in its starting position.

"Come on put your back into it" Richard screamed, knowing he had nothing more to add to shifting the lid.

"What's this thing made of?" Tony asked as he summoned a bit more strength from his powerful shoulders.

"Ahheeeeeee" both Richard & Tony gave the crow bar everything they had. The lid again seemed to be moving and then suddenly popped, a sharp loud crack sounded, as the seal of the lid broke. Balancing between the weight of the lid and the combined body weight of Richard & Tony, they hovered and swayed: both of Tony's feet were clean off the floor. Bouncing slightly the balance became in their favour, the lid gradually moved making a cutting grating sound until the lid was free from its base. A rotten pungent smell met both Richard & Tony's noses simultaneously,

"I smell dead people!" Tony joked who had cleverly adapted a blockbuster films hook line.

"That's not too sweet is it" Richard replied, as they both lowered the crow bar gently to the floor.

Looking at each other for inspiration, Richard's facial expression provided the indication that he was going to venture forward to see what was in the coffin. Although Tony gave a reactive smile he held back and let Richard move on his own. Not entirely comfortable Richard looked round for support, Tony, who was several paces behind gasped,

"What?"

Feeling a little guilty Tony advanced in line with Richard. Almost hand in hand they both tiptoed to the edge of the coffin and lent forward slowly, gradually bringing into view the content of the coffin.

An old and decaying body, who's flesh was still intact, slowly came into view; Richard scrunched his face up as he fought the gagging sensation and controlled the vomit lodged at the back of his throat. Tony, not so in control, turned to his left and proceeded to 'Technicolor Yawn' his lunch up.

Richard looked in amazement at the body before him, although repulsed by what he saw he found he was unable to retreat, glued to the spot where he stood, like a deer caught in headlights. He could not understand how the flesh could be still intact and the clothes the man wore still in a useable condition. Richard focused on an area of the man's face, which was not fully complete. An area of his cheek the size of about a golf ball had rotten away leaving raw flesh, no longer protected by skin, Richard could even make out the small thin blue veins that run through it.

His arms were placed in a crossed peaceful position, Richard looked in detail at its hands, although the flesh still intact the bones could be clearly seen, almost breaking through the skin,

"What's wrong with you?" Tony yelled, breaking the silence and allowing Richard to snap out of his frozen state.

"There's something not right here mate." Richard replied in a calm and informative manner.

"You're damn right" Tony grunted as he aggressively advanced towards the coffin. He grabbed the lid with both hands and started to try and shift it back in position on his own,

"Give me a hand, to put this lid back on, before we both get cursed or something." Tony had forgotten that he was now working overtime and his mate was sitting in a bar on his own feeling very much stood up, Tony's only concern was to get the lid back on, no matter what.

Richard in agreement rushed to the coffin, with adrenalin coursing through his veins he felt he could move the lid single handed, grabbing the lid with a firm grip he acknowledged to Tony,

"On three,"

On three, they both widened their stances and twitched every muscle fibre in their bodies to generate the strength required to move the lid. Slowly but surely the lid moved grating as the mason stone resisted hard against their efforts. Tony keen to get the job done did not ease the pressure he was applying although he was also fighting bringing his dinner up again, as the stench from the corpse filled his lungs. The lid almost closed came to a sharp holt, Tony screamed,

"My finger, my fucking finger, it's trapped, lift the lid up, lift it up!"

Richard rapidly moved to Tony's end of the lid, he grabbed the lid, bending his knees he started to try to lift it,

"Ahhh, sorry mate, I need to get the crow bar,"

"Hurry, I think my finger is coming off!"

Richard looked left to right trying to spot the crow bar leaping over one of the chests he picked the bar up as he slid past it, sliding as if avoiding being 'tagged out' in a baseball game.

Ramming the crow bar underneath the lid Richard prised it up just enough to release Tony's finger. Swiftly Tony pulled his damaged finger out, which had a good-sized chunk missing from it,

"Fuck, fuck!" Tony screamed as he clutched it tight with his other hand.

Looking at the steady stream of blood dripping down Tony's arm, Richard tossed him a slightly used hanky,

"Put that round it, last thing I want is any blood getting near him in there," not knowing just how right, he was.

Using the crow bar, Richard managed to manoeuvre the lid into position then removing the bar quickly allowing the lid to slam shut,

"Let's get out of here!" Richard ordered.

Stopping outside of the container, Tony grabbed one door, Richard the other, in the correct order slamming them firmly shut. Tony very mindful of not trapping any other digits observed Richards movements attentively, ensuring he pushed the lock bar to seal the container without further injury. Hearing the dead lock bolts engage provided comfort to both Richard & Tony. Calmly walking away from the container Richard spoke quietly,

"We speak about this tomorrow, go home, get some rest and make sure you clean that finger up, I don't want you phoning in sick tomorrow."

"No probs, catch ya later." Tony replied as they went their separate ways across the port.

Chapter Two

Dimly lit from distant port lights and separated from the other containers, the newly secured coffin would no longer hold its evil prisoner. Inside the coffin the fresh splash of Tony's blood absorbed by the Counts previously rotting flesh sparked new life into his veins. The splash, sufficient to awake the Count from his long hibernation, sent regeneration signals all over his body. Rapidly healing decayed tissue, electrical pulses scattered over his reforming body. As his flesh magically rebuilt a mild crackling and spiting sound dominated the silence inside the container. After several hours the electrical pulses stopped and for a moment all was still. An almighty bolt of lightning lit the Portsmouth sky above, immediately followed by an earth shaking crack of thunder, as the calm again restored the Count opened his eyes.

Licking his lips the Count slowly uncrossed his arms and cricked his neck both sides, pausing for a second he looked around the inside of the lid, without taking a further breath he simultaneously thrust both arms upwards palms open. The 300kg lid was of no match to the power of the Count, breaking into large segments which fell to the floor around the coffin. The Count sat up methodically and muttered,

"You will no longer imprison me."

Seamlessly, the Count glided over the contours of the coffin, to settle on the container floor. Hungry from his long rest he walked to a chest filled with blood and picked up a vial. Popping the cork with one swift stroke of his thumb he paused, almost as if he really did not want to drink it,

'I do hate cold blood'.

After devouring the content of one chest, he wiped a trickle of blood from the side of his mouth, content he was now full.

Turning to the direction of the doors, he extended his forefinger and pointed his long fingernail at the doors. As he did so the doors chattered and flexed, the lock on the outside also caught in the Counts power popped open just as the doors flew wide open. With a chest of money under one arm, the Count stepped outside the container.

Deeply breathing in the cold Portsmouth air he smiled, rolling his eyes and baring his normal teeth he felt free and ready to fulfil his purpose. Closing his eyes he raised his head towards the bright moon and concentrated his thoughts. Thousands of images flashed into his mind, pausing for a 1000th of a second and then passing to reveal the next, these images were in the form of a plan view similar to a snap shot taken from a satellite camera. Eventually the images stopped and locked on a location of a manor house in the New Forest. Taking a further deep breath the Count spun on his feet a quarter of a turn and disappeared, his image collapsing from top to bottom, leaving behind nothing but a small trace of moving dust. Materialising in his chosen destination, he looked around his new home, a grand old manor with boarded windows and little natural light,

"Perfect."

Performing this magical form of transportation several times the Count collected the remaining chests. Aware that his appearance was not both modern nor attractive he knew he would be dining on cold stale blood for the meantime but also knew it would not be long before he would feast on warm pulsing nectar.

Richard arrived at work as usual 30 minutes early, a creature of habit he liked to enjoy a coffee and read the paper before starting his day. His desk a normal 'guys' desk organised in places but with paperwork, which regularly moved from tray to tray to by the keyboard, by the mouse mat etc, etc.

Richard looked around the dull decorated office and thought,

'I have got to get another job.'

Looking back down at his paper he tried reading the 1st couple of lines again but found himself drifting into memories of yesterday's events. Looking at his watch again he wondered if Tony would be in or whether he would phone in sick.

"Morning Richard," said a colleague who was just finishing the night shifts security.   "Morning Geoff, fancy a cupper?"

"Yeah in a min, have you spoken to Alan yet?"
"No Why?"
"You were the last one to inspect the single container on the Far East side weren't you?"
"Why?" Richard asked.
"It was broken into last night all that is left is an old smashed coffin."

Richard wanted to ask many questions but decided against this and bit his lip,

"Do you take milk in your tea?" Richard again looked at his watch and thought 'Come on Tony hurry up.'

Tony not a punctual chap arrived surprisingly early and broke the awkward silence, "Two sugars for me, seeing's you're in the chair."

Pleased to see Tony, Richard did not argue and did as he was asked.

Richard waited for the office to clear from its usual morning burst of staff before explaining what he had been told. Tony mindful he was seriously due a windup played on him thought long and hard before answering,

"Pull the other one, I may look wet behind the ears but you seriously will have to get up a bit earlier Pops to get me."

Richard a little stressed, as Alan his boss was shortly due in snapped,

"No you fucking moron I am not pissing about, I am serious, it's all gone except the coffin!"

A question, which Richard had already asked himself, came from Tony's lips

"What about the dead guy?"

"I don't know, I really don't, I am going to go over to take a look, hopefully before Alan gets in, are you coming?" Before Tony could even think he answered,

"Yeah man."

Grabbing their coats they made their way out of the office.

As they approached the abandoned container, Tony looked at Richard and admitted to himself that he was feeling quite nervous. Stopping in the opening of the container they looked for signs of anything out of the ordinary or suspicious. Their attention was drawn to the lid, which lay in several large slabs approximately two feet from the coffin,

"Who could have lifted that clean off?" Richard questioned,

"I don't know but fucked if I want to meet them in a dark alley!"

Walking slowly and unsure, the pair moved towards the coffin, checking around them as they progressed. Now in front of the tomb both were surprised to see the body missing, well surprised as well as worried.

"Do you think the thieves took the body?" Tony asked in a timid voice.

"Well either they did or it got up and walked out and unlocked steel doors from the inside!" Richard replied sarcastically and then looked at Tony with a puzzled face as if what he had just said could be an option,

"What we gonna do Ricky? What's on the paperwork? Who else knows what was actually in here?"

"Woah down with all the questions Tony, I have not really thought this through yet, let's get back to the office and logically go through this. How are you fixed today? Can you spare me an hour to sit down and chat this through?"

"Mate, of course I can spare the time, I'm gonna be handing my notice in, in about 10 mins, so will be totally free after that."

Not sure if Tony was joking around Richard replied,
"11am ok with you?"
"Yeah that's cool."

Tony arrived at Richard's desk promptly at 10.58am; Richard had thought of nothing else for the last hour, yet when Tony asked,

"What's the plan boss?"

"I really don't know what to do for the best," was Richard's reply.

"Tony have a seat. The way I look at it is only you and me know what was in there, I think. I broke the seal off of the lock and the security guard did not mention what was stolen and the paperwork was very vague. So I guess if you and I can keep this quiet and our detail straight then we should be ok. What do you think?"

Tony not really understanding the implications of telling the truth was convinced Richards plan was a good one,

"I'm cool with that,"

They spent the next 40 minutes ensuring their detail was watertight when their meeting was disturbed by an email from Alan summoning Richard to his office.

After the weird chain of events Tony sat at the bar of a trendy pub waiting for his buddy to turn up, the one he had stood up the night before. Tapping the polished bronze handrail of the bar to the beat of the music, he glanced at the time shown on the big LCD screen, which was providing the music source. His buddy was similar to himself and not known for being on time was already 35 minutes late.

"Another pint please" Tony said in a raised voice, to get the bar mans attention. As the barman started to pour Tony's pint a familiar voice spoke from behind him, "Make that two mate" Jason, Tony's buddy arrived.

"Sorry I am late man, the Mrs started going on at me that I was out last night with you and was I really meeting up with you or was I having an affair etc, so I had to sort that out before I could leave."

"Yeah sorry about that Jay, something last minute meant I had to work late, did you get my text?"

"Yeah got it, all ok? It is not like you to work a second of overtime"

"Not going to be making a habit out of it either, want some crisps?" Tony asked as he neatly swerved the question.

As the night progressed, the idea of hitting a nightclub appealed to Jason, after all he was already in the doghouse and far too drunk to drive so might as well go the full hog.

"Shall we hit Cinderella's buddy?"

Tony a single man thought this to be a fantastic idea,

"Yes mate, I was going to phone in sick tomorrow anyway"

Being a Thursday night the club was not at full capacity which allowed the boys to get served easily and window shop for available women. Happy to prop up the bar they both stood with their backs to it, jigging their heads to the beat, whilst being very careful not to spill their beer. Unable to form any constructive conversation over the volume of the music they scanned the dance floor for babes, occasionally looking at each other to acknowledge a sweet find.

Jason a happily married man still fancied himself as a bit of a stud and always liked the challenge of pulling a younger hotty. This was something that bothered Tony, as he was very unhappy being single and aspired to Jason as having 'it all' and could see where Jill, Jason's wife was coming from. Tony took a sip from his cold bottle of beer and as he did he looked down the bottle keeping his eye on the dance floor. A young lady probably about 23 years old mingled from the dance floor and made her way towards the bar, Tony could not help thinking,

'Wow look at the body on that.'

As she got closer to the bar Tony started to feel a little uncomfortable, as he had worked out that she was coming over to them not the bar. Panicking of what he was going to say to the incredibly attractive lady who was wearing not more than a belt and a vest zooming towards him, his panic was over, as Jason extending his left arm inviting the lady in his direction and smoothly said,

"Do you know you can tell a lot about a person from their writing?"

The lady looked at Jason, smiled and positioned herself close to Jason. Tony knew Jason, a legend when it came to the ladies, could not fail and would most definitely be leaving with her.

Understanding that Jason's efforts and attention would now be with the hot babe, he would require to amuse himself. Looking around the club he wondered if he was getting a bit old for the club scene and hoped a stunning girl, the lady of his dreams would materialise and sweep him of his feet. Taking a large swig of beer, he found that he was quite impressed with the laser & strobe light show and wondered how they worked without anyone operating them. Snapping out of his inquisitive mood he quickly realised with thoughts like that he stood no chance of pulling tonight. The time now was 1.15am, Tony felt relaxed about calling it a night, he would of course have told Jason that he was leaving but Jason was nowhere to be found. Tired, Tony did not fancy checking out the obvious places Jason would have taken the young lass for a quick shag.

Literally stumbling out the doors of the club, Tony realised that he was quite wasted and his thoughts quickly turned to seeking a kebab or equivalent stodge. Walking the best he could he tried to maintain a normal straight line walk in the direction of the kebab shop. This was proving harder than he initially imagined, bouncing just slightly off a shop window he stopped for a second and shut both eyes to focus his motor skills. The kebab shop was in sight but his bladder bursting with excess lager was pulling rank. Ducking down a side alley, Tony checked for both cameras and other people, although he was very drunk he did not wish to get caught on camera doing his business.

Finding a suitable spot Tony removed his manhood and released what seemed several litres of purified lager.

Still a kid at heart Tony pretended that the high pressure jet was a laser cannon and made noises to that effect as he manoeuvred his magic wand. Repositioning his feet to avoid the miniature version of the River Thames he was creating, he moved his shoulders and juddered in a way as if someone had walked over his grave. Finishing his wee he gave his usual three shakes and then paused for a second and gave two further more. He had this strange theory that if he pretended to put his willy away and then gave it a further couple of shakes he would trick it so not to drip in his pants. Pulling his zip up and turning to exit the alley, his face which was now content suddenly became white, his eyes widened and an expression of sheer terror dominated his face.

The Count spoke calmly,
"Tony, I believe?" speechless Tony's mouth opened, his head violently vibrated but no words came out.
"Thank you for my new lease of life, for this, I am eternally grateful."
Still unable to speak and frozen to the spot where he stood he pulled a nervous half-hearted grin. He knew that this compliment could not be a good thing; the Count took a smooth step towards Tony, gently extending his arm in a non-threatening manner. Tony knew he had nowhere to go with the wall he had just wee'd up against behind him. Cringing and shaking like a frightened puppy Tony closed his eyes slightly; he could feel the Count's hand close to his face. Caressing Tony's face the Count spoke calmly and clearly,
"Now in return, I am going to give you the gift of eternal life,"

Before Tony could work out what had just been explained to him, his thoughts were startled by immense pain, as the Counts inch long fingernail pierced his neck and lodged firmly into his jugular vein. Naturally reacting, Tony raised his hand to grab the Counts arm but stopped as the Count lightly twisted his deeply embedded finger. "Ahh, What do you want from me? You Freak!" Tony squealed in a cross of anger and pain,

"You my friend now have a serious decision to make. The choice you have to make is simple, I can remove my finger from your neck and your blood will leave your body at such a rate, you will certainly die, or you can agree to stand by my side and I will give you a life of eternity." With this the Counts eyes widened and he moved his face closer to Tony's. Tony knew that he was not going to have long to think about this, reacted by saying,

"You could use some tick tacks or something for starters, I don't really see I have much of a choice, I don't understand what is involved with standing by your side and I don't want the last thing I see is my claret spurting all over the place. Can I phone a friend?"

The Count remained silent, slightly tilting his head, after further silence it was broken by Tony,

"I thought not. I guess option 2 is the most appealing at this moment in time."

With that the Count smiled, his facial expression resembled a cat who had got the cream,

"Well done, a good answer."

With his eyes Tony repeatedly flicked them left to indicate to the Count his finger was still firmly embedded in his neck.

"Oh Tony I am a man of my word."

Tony felt a hot pulse like tingling surround the Counts finger. As the Count removed his finger, electrostatic sparks zapped a small radius around Tony's wound, quartarising it as the finger departed. The tingling sensation continued and contaminated Tony's entire body, as he worked out that whatever the Count had done was now in his blood stream. Adjusting to this new sensation, Tony asked,
"Do I get any special powers with this new job?"
"Unfortunately not my friend, you are however immortal a gift that some relish and others demise. Your life can only be taken by myself. So obey me and you will live forever."
"That doesn't seem so bad." Tony replied,
"We have much work to do. You have a busy day ahead of you." The Count said in a commanding voice, whilst rolling his fingers as if tumbling a coin, they both disappeared into thin air.

Chapter Three

Tony found himself materialising in the Counts new home, briefly looking around to take in where he was he gagged and regurgitated a large mouthful of sick.

"It is common for that to happen, the first several teleports," advised the Count.

"You will need to rest. Teleporting applies great demands on your body."

"That's one to add to the list of life experiences, supernatural jetlag." Tony muttered under his breath.

Looking around the empty house Tony asked,

"Where do I sleep?"

"For the moment the floor will provide a place of rest, we will improve upon this very soon. Now rest."

Tony awoke from a restless night's sleep, aching from the hard wood floor, subconsciously scratching his neck where the counts finger had previously impaled him. Not pleased with the taste in his mouth Tony looked around to try and locate the kitchen as he really needed a drink. His view was obstructed by the Count,

"Morning Vamps, I thought you guys didn't rise in the daytime."

"You have lots to learn my friend, lots. Now listen we have much to do and little time. Firstly you need to take small amounts of my dollars and exchange them at the bank for the currency of this country. Explain you were left these old notes in a will, they are still a usable currency so if in small amounts you should have no problems. Do this at many banks to clear one chest, come back to me when you have done this. Feed yourself and purchase supplies that you require to exist here. I will warn you, you do not possess my powers but you are immortal, you will have no reflection, you will no longer be able to view your own appearance."

Tony a chap who naturally liked to shop liked the idea of his first assignment and thought,

'Maybe this won't be so bad.'

Tony did as he was told and visited as many different banks. He could not believe how easy it was to 'launder' the dollars and finally returned to the house a rich man. He had made a couple of stops as told to purchase items that he needed to exist, food, clothes, toiletries and mobile phones. The LCD TV, PC, beds and furniture etc, would be delivered as and when. Tony thought he didn't have to live in the dark ages and Vamp could do with being brought up to date.

Tony organised his purchases when he felt he was not alone, the Count stood behind him and calmly asked,

"I take that all went well?"

"Yes Boss, really had a result," before Tony could finish his sentence the Count interrupted,

"Well done, you have a very busy day ahead of you tomorrow. I want you to put your house up for rent, organise the utilities for here and purchase transport for yourself, nothing too elaborate, nothing that will draw attention. I will be out tonight, please feed and rest well."

With that the Count turned and walked gracefully into another room. Tony muttered,

"Anything else?" it was quite late and Tony knew to achieve all of the Counts wishes he would need to get an early night.

As Richard tied the handles of the pedal bin liner, he carefully avoided the tomato sauce, which somehow had managed to jump from inside the bag to the handles. He shouted to Pam his wife,

"Just taking the rubbish out, it is bin day tomorrow isn't it?"

The silent reply was not uncommon as Pam often ignored Richard.

"I'll take that as a yes then darling!" Richard sarcastically muttered.

Careful not to tear the bin liner as he negotiated the kitchen door, Richard made his way outside to the wheelie bin. The wheelie bin was neatly positioned down the side of Richards's back garden shed and parameter fence. Looking up as he walked towards the bin he waved his free left hand above his head, enticing the PIR flood light to come on.

'Bloody useless thing, one day I will break my neck doing this. I think next week Pam can do the bins.'

Grabbing the handle of the wheelie bin, Richard pulled it to ease the bin from its home. He knew it was not really full so the fact he could not move it concerned him. Giving it one final almighty tug Richard could really not understand why the bin would not budge. Walking back towards the house Richard frantically waved his arms trying to work out where the beams of the PIR would be to activate the 500w halogen bulb.

For a brief second the garden became fully lit as the flood light sprang into life. As quickly as it had beamed with almost daylight energy it again became dark. A loud pop broke the late evening silence as it became clear to Richard that the bulb had just blown.

Reaching into his trouser pocket Richard removed his house keys and advanced towards the shed. Fumbling in the dark he tried to locate the keyhole of the padlock, which secured the shed. After several attempts he successfully engaged the key and twisted it anti clockwise to unlock it. Opening the shed door only slightly, he felt around for a torch which was cunningly positioned alone on the first shelf near to the door just for emergencies such as this. As his hand roamed over the objects of the shelf he knocked a large tin of WD40 which fell to the floor.

'Bugger, I must have moved the torch,'

Pushing the door wider he stepped into the shed scanning the shelves for an object that's silhouette resembled a torch. Locating the torch and pressing the on button a dim light emitted from it, indicating to Richard that the batteries were very low. Stepping back out of the shed he pointed the dull beam at the wheelie bin, firstly

Man's Natural Predator

aiming at the wheels to understand if there was a large stone or some other obstruction stopping it moving. Moving closer to the bin he was convinced that he could not see any obstruction, slowly moving the beam up the bin he noticed a flesh like colour on the other handle to which he was previously pulling. Jerking the torch beam back to this position he looked intensely, although the light was a dull yellow he could clearly make out the long nails and fingers of the Count. Rapidly moving the torch light along the contour of the Counts arm he then aimed the light where he estimated his face to be. As the torch light settled on the face of the Count Richard had roughly around half a second to absorb the image in front of him.

The Count let off a piercing hiss, his eyes turned cat like and glowed white, quickly lunging forward, his mouth wide open targeting Richards neck.

As the fangs of the Count sunk deep into Richards neck, Richard realised the shocking different face of the Count would be the last thing he would ever see.

The Count thrashed his bite from left to right opening the wound to Richard's jugular allowing maximum blood flow, as he did so the Count sounded a smothered growl similar to that of a dog killing a rabbit. The pain Richard felt was like nothing else he had ever experienced, his body locked in an epileptic spasm, fingers extended wide. He could physically feel his body being totally drained of the very important plasma fluid needed to maintain existence. The final sensation of pins and needles in his feet provided Richard with the indication that he had little time left, rolling his eyes back into their sockets, his mouth wide with pain he tried to scream but instead a gasp of warm air exhaled as Richards major organs failed, Richard was no more.

As Richard's body became limp the Count released his fatal bite and slowly drew away, momentarily shutting his eyes with content he savoured the taste of his first live feed.

Placing a hand underneath Richard's armpit the Count zoomed upwards into the night sky taking Richard with him. Travelling at a speed in excess of 200mph the Count flew over houses and treetops until he reached a large lake several miles from Richard's house. Focusing his powers he hovered about ten feet over the calm water, releasing his grip on Richard, Richard's lifeless body fell, slowly spiralling as it plummeted towards the water. A loud splash sounded as his body impacted with the water's surface. The Count hovered a little longer whilst he watched Richard's body sink into the cold dark water, then without trace vanished into the night skies.

Chapter Four

The following day, Tony worked hard to achieve the Counts tasks, he could not believe with a few phone calls and giving over his bank details all the utilities needed were confirmed and being connected later that day. His house would be ready for leasing/renting within two weeks. The estate agent suggested a quick lick of paint to freshen up the property would increase the probability of securing a tenant quickly. Once the electric was connected all that he had to do was purchase a 2nd hand car. He decided to chance the electric man not coming for a little while and popped to the local newsagents to get the auto trader.

On his return he noticed the van of the electric man,

"Shit, always the way," running towards the van he hoped that the engineer was not completing an abandoned visit card.

"Hello, Hello!"

Tony aimed his voice at the recently jet washed van, looking in the driver's seat to try and get the engineers attention. Jerking his head back Tony was surprised there was no sign of the engineer. Tony erratically thought,

'Oh I hope Vamps hasn't eaten him before he turned the power on!'

Running to the door which was wide open Tony thought,

'This doesn't look good' and entered.

Just as Tony rushed into the house he was greeted by the engineer coming out.

"Afternoon sir, all done, just need a signature from you and I will be on my way."

"Of course, no problem, thank you for getting this done so efficiently."

Tony took the form, his hands shaking, the form vibrated at the top. This went unnoticed by the engineer as he inputted the details of the finished job on his portable PDA.

"Nice gaff," the engineer added as he took the form back and separated its multiple layers and handing Tony the top copy.

"It's not too shabby," was all Tony could think of to say.

The engineer started to return to his van, when both of their attention jolted to the direction of the sound of a large lorry coming up the drive. Working out that he needed to move his van out of the way, the engineer accelerated towards his van placing his hand over his right shoulder to gesture farewell.

Looking at the sign writing on the van Tony's face lit up as he realised it was the LCD TV, PC etc. Tony thought with the luck I am having I might put the lottery on tomorrow.

Checking the itinerary, Tony happy all items were present thought,

'Now how does all this go together then?' when his thoughts were disturbed,

"Tony, what has been delivered?"

"Ahh, well I know you have been locked up for a bit and all that but these items will really be useful, trust me." Tony had lost his spit and felt very nervous that Vamps reaction was not going to be a good one.

"I do trust you Tony. I do not think you would try to deceive me, that would of course be very foolish. When you have finished with all of this please explain to me what it all does and I am sure I will be pleased."

In an attempt to break the mood Tony replied,

"And the beds are being delivered tomorrow. That's good news eh?"

Slightly shaking his head in despair the Count said nothing, turned and left the room.

Tony, excited with the boxes in front of him, decided to skip his evening meal and construct the technological gadgetry. After several hours, Tony was convinced all was connected correctly and boldly pressed the on button of the 42" LCD TV. The screen energised went from a dull black to a clear light blue, a white message blinked in different positions across the obscene screen 'no signal'.

"Bollocks!"

Now really annoyed Tony rapidly scratched his head with his left hand, whilst repositioning his manhood with his right. This was an old habit he could not seem to shake and often found himself fiddling with his bits and bobs when serious concentration was involved.

Tracing the wires from the set top box to the back of the TV he noticed the power lead of the set top box was not plugged in. Enthusiastic he had found the problem, Tony plugged in the set top box. Immediately the TV sprung into life for a brief second before performing an automatic channel search. Patiently waiting Tony stood with baited breath, after about 45 seconds the picture displayed BBC1.

"Excellent, I'm back in the game."

The news broadcaster chanted on about the same old politics, which normally dominated the news with the addition of America's announcing its war on Terrorism. Tony pointed the remote towards the TV increasing the volume and adjusting the picture characteristics to suit the lighting of the dull room. Pressing exit from the menu page the picture shone vibrant and clear. Admiring the quality of the picture and experimenting with a couple of screen formats, Tony was not really paying too much attention to the detail of the news.

The sound of the back of the TV remote smashing off its fixings onto the old wooden floor amplified over the volume of the TV. Tony stood with his mouth wide open and vacantly stared at the regional reporter as he absorbed the pictures of a body being pulled from a lake. Although the body was well hidden from the cameras and wrapped in body bag type blankets, Tony recognised the person to be Richard.

"Yes Fiona, another brutal stabbing, to bring Portsmouth's count up to an astonishing three this week alone. Although not confirmed it is believed that the murder weapon used is a six inch nail and was stabbed repeatedly in to the victims neck. Police have notified the victim's relatives and are not disclosing the victims name at this stage, a full investigation is being launched. Back to you, Fiona."

The news presenter paused for a second to show her concern for yet another murder and then continued,

"Tony Blair has today announced...."

Devastated by this news, Tony stood motionless, like a robot that was being rebooted. His blank facial expression occasionally altered by the necessity to blink. As he stood his emotions went from deep sorrow and loss, to anger, to rage as he worked out that this was no street stabbing but the Vamps work. Clenching his left fist tight, he could feel his heart rate increase and his breathing deepen. Turning his head to see over his shoulder he turned and stomped off to find the Count. As the manor house had over thirty rooms this was no mean feat. Crossing the Kitchen from the entertainments room or the 'Command Centre' as Tony had named it, he was met by the Count.

"What seems to be the problem?" the Count asked knowingly

"You killed Richard, didn't you, you mother fu..." before Tony could finish his sentence, the Count calmly spoke

"I understand your loss Tony," opening his arms in a friendly gesture and moving around Tony in a circling motion, he continued,

"Only you and Richard knew of my existence and this is something I require to protect, I am sorry he was someone you knew, I know this is difficult for you to understand. You yourself will require to slowly detach from your friends and family without raising any suspicions, the cause that we fight is a very lonely one."

"What cause are you talking about? What, you feel a little peckish so someone has to lose their life is that a cause is it?"

Walking to Tony the Count smoothly placed his arm around Tony's shoulders and said,

"Walk with me, I had hoped to explain this to you later but I feel now is the time."

Now very worried, Tony's anger suddenly turned to self preservation and he became very mindful that the Count could most probably rip him to pieces without even breaking into a sweat.

"Of course, please explain away."

As they romantically strolled across the kitchen towards the main front door the Count said,

"From the dawn of mankind, I have been in existence, placed on this earth to keep the population of humans in balance with the circle of life. Everything has its natural predator, a lamb has the wolf, a chicken has the fox, need I go on? The way, in which I feed, is to man barbaric, although to man the way a Lion brings down its kill is perfectly acceptable. I have never been a man, I am a Demon and I have roamed the earth for many, many thousands of years and have constantly battled humans trying to eradicate me and my children from this earth. I cannot be vanished, silver bullets, steaks to my heart, holy water do not kill me they only force me into hiding. I always return in one shape, form or another. I only feed at night to keep my identity and existence secret. The claims of bursting into flames if daylight hits my skin are not true. Like every animal I need my rest so choose to rest during the day. I have been gifted with immense powers, which I only am blessed with this, is not passed on to my children or humans that I turned.

"Turned? What is turned" Tony asked, whilst thinking to himself,

'I guess you've been waiting a really long time to get this lot off your chest.'

"Turned, is when instead of totally feeding, I leave just a little blood, just enough to maintain life. I inject a small amount of my blood from my fangs, which quickly alters their DNA makeup, which over only a few days turns their stomach to enable the digestion of blood and grow the retractable fangs they need to feed. I usually 'Turn' people whose lives have no real meaning, people that are more of a strain on the world than they actually give back."

"Wow, you should put that on TV, you would probably get more votes than Tony Blair!"

Confused the Count asked, "What's a TV?"

"Ah yes, you did ask me to show you what was in the boxes once it was all set up, let me know when you are ready and I'll give you a run down. Do you have time now?"

"Sorry Tony, I require to now go out, can you present your purchases to me later tomorrow?"

"Not a problem, should also have the internet working by then."

Not knowing what Tony was talking about, the Count nodded to accept he had heard him but couldn't help think he was not going to be any clearer after Tony's presentation.

Hungry the Count decided to pop out for a bite, he was mindful that his attire and old-fashioned dialect would draw unnecessary attention and hesitated,

'Shall I have cold blood for one more night? NO tonight it begins!'

Chapter Five

Hitching her left stocking up slightly, Melinda rocked from her left foot to her right, she found that this passed the time and showed off her perfectly formed long legs.

Looking at her cheap imitation Rolex, the time read 10:45pm. By now she would have normally earned in the region of £350 but for some reason business was slow. Worried how she was going to pay for her next fix, she removed a silver decorative mirror from her handbag and reapplied her lush red lipstick. She could only imagine that she was not looking her best and therefore this was the reason for the quiet takings.

Melinda a very beautiful lady unfortunately had strayed to the dark side and formed a serious cocaine habit. Unfastening another button of her Spanish looking white blouse, she revealed a little more of her olive skin cleavage. Melinda, naturally blessed with firm plump breasts, knew that revealing her secret weapons would certainly liven up the evening.

The Count materialised several meters behind Melinda in a bus stop. As the ash like smoke cleared around the Count, he stood momentarily and surveyed the area, calculating his odds of being detected. Confident he had appeared unnoticed he smoothly walked toward Melinda. Creeping right up behind her, his crutch almost touching her arse, the Count positioned his head just over her shoulder and whispered into her ear.

"What is a beautiful young lady like yourself doing working the streets?"

Startled, Melinda leapt forward struggling to balance on her five-inch stilettos heels. Looking over her shoulder she gasped,

"Watch it you freak, you scared the shit out of me!"

"For this I am sorry, the last thing on my mind is frightening you. How much is your services for the entire night?"

"You could not afford it handsome, what about a blowjob instead?"

The count took a minute to ponder her answer and smiled. He liked the fact that he still appeared as a good-looking man. Being 6'2" heavily built, with a trim waste and the facial similarities of George Clooney may have had a lot to do with it.

"No seriously Melinda, how much?"

"Well including hotel room for the entire night you are looking at £1,000 easy." Thinking he will never go for this, it suddenly dawned on her, how did he know my name?

"£1,000 it is then I will pay you £500 now and £500 in the morning. That is if you can survive the pace."

Reaching into his jacket pocket he pulled out a roll of fifty pound notes which Melinda quickly worked out to be in the region of about three grand. Using his thumb and forefinger he rolled off ten notes. His long nails, which proved very useful in many ways, made this easy task look quite cumbersome. Slowly extending his arm he offered the money to Melinda, she could not help but notice his claw like finger nails.

"I hope you are not intending to use those nails on my back? Mr," she expressed as she took possession of the money.

"I will try my best not to hurt you, I promise."

With that the Counts face broke a cheeky smile, which Melinda found quite irresistibly charming.

"Is the hotel near?" The Count enquired.

"Yes, yes just around the corner, calm down tiger you have all night."

As they walked in the direction of the hotel, Melinda put her arm around the Count's waste and in an impressed voice asked,

"Do you work out?"

Not understanding the question the count replied,

"I work all over the place but mainly outside."

Looking at the Count with a face of astonishment, she was unsure if he was trying to be funny or if he was just simply a rich moron. Business being business, she laughed in a false outlandish cackle and said,

"You're so funny, stop you're killing me."

The Count looked deep into Melinda's clear blue eyes and said,

"Your craving is strong, I understand what it is like to constantly crave, we need to feed your addiction, I want you to enjoy tonight."

Amazed at how he knew, Melinda remained silent, unsure that her client may be a cop.

The silence continued for several minutes until the Count spoke,

"Please wait here, I will not be long."

Before Melinda had a chance to answer, the Count was already half way across the road heading towards a lad on the opposite path. As the Count got close to this man he lunged his shoulder firmly into the other mans.

"Watch it pal." The man grunted.

"I need some of your amphetamines please." Ordered the Count holding the man firmly in position with one arm.

"Get the fuck out of here, before I slash ya." the man warned, a metallic sound backed up his bold statement, as his flick knife locked into position.

"I did ask nicely," the count calmly uttered, as he wrenched the man's arm up and clean out of its socket.

Briefly the man's feet dangled, as the Count held him several inches off of the pavement. Frantically with his good arm the man fumbled in his coat pocket, removing a good size bag of white powder.

"Take it, take it." The man yelled in absolute agony.

Gently lowering the man back to the ground the Count took the bag and released his grasp. The man petrified reacted as any normal man would and ran like the wind.

Returning to Melinda the count spoke in an inviting voice,

"We are now ready, please lead on."

After seeing him lift a 14 stone man clean off of the floor, she decided that 'wise cracks' were not appropriate and simply nodded.

A little on edge Melinda looked around the hotel room, not sure if her client was safe she weighed up the remaining £500 versus legging it. Her gut instinct was telling her to 'do a runner' but was overruled by the Count placing the bag of cocaine in her view on the sideboard. The Count looked at Melinda and through his eyes he saw a thermal image of her body, her blood pulsing around her veins. He could see her nervous system was screaming for a further fix.

"Take a small amount, not all of it, you can then relax and enjoy the evening."

Melinda's body aching for a fix, she advanced towards the bag, similar to a starving dog, she ripped the bag open single handed. With the other she found her inhaler from her handbag. Organising the powder into two long lines, she snorted both of them up one nostril.

Taking a second she breathed in deeply, her face content as her addiction became tamed.

Understanding that Melinda would probably not be able to resist the remaining content of the bag, the Count picked it up and proceeded towards the toilet.

"I'm going to take a shower, please feel free to help yourself to any refreshments."

Melinda, not used to clients actually caring for her needs found this quite novel and slipped into the role of being a mistress to a wealthy tycoon.

Laying spread eagled on the bed her eyes became very heavy, fighting to keep them open they flickered. In conjunction with the cocaine, she drifted in and out of consciousness.

The Count refreshed from his shower returned into the room wearing just a hotel towel. He paused to admire Melinda's beauty, before creeping upon the bed with stealth like precision. Gently he positioned himself over her, supporting his body weight with his arms. The Count, ravenous, needed to feed but also wished to enjoy what he had paid for. Slowly lowering himself into position he opened his mouth to reveal his fully extracted fangs. A clear droplet of local anaesthetic formed on each fang, as he lowered his head alongside her neck. Gently kissing her neck in several places he paused, allowing the anaesthetic to take effect, before piercing her skin with his fangs. Controlling himself not to over feed, the Count drank slowly and gently. The cocaine, which was present in her bloodstream, had no effect on the Count as he was immune to any such impurities. Slowly pulling away from her neck, his fangs broke free from her skin. His fangs emitted a small amount of serum, which quickly clotted her blood.

Sitting beside Melinda, still only wearing a towel, the Count looked at her and reminisced of all the beautiful relationships he had experienced over the many thousands of years. Gently running his forefinger claw along her arm he decided to allow her to sleep for a while.

Lifting her head off the pillow Melinda grasped her head, this was a normal reaction as she was used to having some form of hangover/headache. This one was of course a lot worse. Melinda had been a sleep for only three hours but the need to replenish her fluids woke her.

"Drink my sweet." The Count calmly spoke, as he handed her a large glass of water.

Very un-lady like she drank vigorously, making an occasional slurping sound. Taking her time to wake up, she looked at the Count, impressed with his chiselled rack of abs and his developed chest she turned her attention to why she was there in the first place.

"Would you mind excusing me, whilst I freshen up?"

"Why of course not, I will be waiting for you right here."

Returning to the bedroom, Melinda started undressing as she walked. A true pro she made the simple things such as unfastening her blouse, look very sexy. Slipping her mini skirt over the contours of her peach like bottom she lowered herself slightly to allow the skirt to rest on the floor, straightening back to her normal stance as she stepped out of the skirt. Her stockings, which were white lace, complimented her olive skin and long legs. Removing one of her high heel shoes, the Count intercepted.

"No please leave them on."

Melinda a naturally horny woman spoke in a seductive voice,

"Whatever turns you on is alright with me."

Replacing her shoe she stopped at the end of the bed. Placing one hand firmly on the bed she lowered herself and looked the Count directly in the eyes. Licking her lips she slowly raised her opposing knee onto the bed and continued towards the Count like a stalking cat. Extending her hand she caressed the inside of the Counts leg, her touch gentle but confident in its intention. Passing her hand lightly over the hairs of his legs, he smiled and slumped heavily back into the pillows. It had been a long time since he had been touched with such affection. Lifting her hand from his skin she slowly glided over the hotel white towel. Hesitating and teasing, she tiptoed her fingers around the area which held the towel in place. Advancing her body in a seductive manner, she leant forward and placed a soft moist kiss in the area of his belly button. Rolling her tongue around the perimeter of his navel, she looked up at him and smiled with an expression that she was about to give him the ride of his life.

Melinda placed strategic kisses firstly on his midriff, then his chest and finally settling on his neck. Landing her bottom lip first she closed the kiss and gently puckered for a brief second, leaving a slight moist area behind as she moved onto the next kiss.

Rising from his neck her mouth millimetres from his, they paused briefly. She looked him in the eyes with a loving look and proceeded with a passionate deep kiss.

Whilst they felt each other's passion through their tongues, Melinda unfastened his towel. Slowly her hand felt its way towards his genitals, her hand gently grasping his semi hard penis. Smoothly jerking her hand she gently stroked him to a rock hard 8" member.

Man's Natural Predator

Breaking away from their kiss, she kissed his body like before but in reverse order eventually stopping at his genitals. Licking the base of his penis, she turned her hand action into a corkscrew type motion but only passing over his top section. Widening her tongue, she moved it up to the top of his penis, circling around his rim with the tip of her tongue. Opening her mouth, she took his manhood in, swallowing his entire 8 inches. One of her specialities was being able to perform this manoeuvre, she found unlike others she did not gag. After holding this position for a little while she began a smooth rhythm up and down on his shaft.

Proficient at what she did, the Count found himself catching his breath, rolling his eyes in ecstasy but wished to return the pleasure. Taking her fine firm bottom in one hand he gently moved her into the 69 position and reciprocated oral sex. Having a long tongue and the knowledge of a woman's anatomy, Melinda in a sexy voice cried,

"Yes there, that's it."

With the Counts many years of experience Melinda climaxed in seconds, squirting her juices all over the Counts face. Unable to continue with her task she juddered as the sensations overwhelmed her body. Catching her breath she opened her eyes and moved off the Count.

"Hmmm, you are a bad boy but I like it."

Still very hard and far from finished the Count took her by the waist and positioned her facing the headboard. Taking a hold of the headboard with both hands Melinda positioned her legs wide to allow the Count to enter.

With his heart rate elevated he nestled up behind her, taking his time to ensure his entry was correct. Placing his tip in her vagina and slowly entering her, he asked,

"Is that ok?"

"Hmm, yes it feels fine."

Keeping his pace slow and gentle he took her breasts in both hands gently removing them from her bra. Kneading them with a soft touch he moved them in motion with his rhythm. Mindful of his long nails he used his thumb and forefinger to gently massage her nipples, whilst placing passionate kisses in her shoulder blades.

In line with his inward stroke Melinda let out a sharp cry of delight. Increasing his pace he thrust his penis into Melinda harder, taking his hands back to her hips to steady his position.

"Faster, faster!" Melinda begged

Increasing his rhythm and penetration, his balls slapped her hard with every downward thrust.

"Yes, Yes, Yes, Yeeeeeeesss!" Melinda cried as she had another orgasm.

Pausing his momentum, whilst she enjoyed and finished her climax, the Count started to slowly start his motion again. Leaning forward and widening his legs he kept the rhythm slow but increased the force of his thrust, he whispered in her ear.

"You are so beautiful and will remain so for many, many years. You can now finally enjoy your life and will be respected from now on. Over the next several days, things will happen that you will not understand, just close your eyes and think of me and I will be with you.

You have a new addiction now. Please look after and bring my child up with love, understand his desire and differences. My love will always be with you."

As he whispered the last few words, he rammed his penis hard into her releasing an immense thick jet of warm sperm.

Feeling his ejaculation, Melinda thought,

'Normally I insist on using a condom, what happened there, did I take my pill this morning?'

A little disturbed by what she had just had whispered in her ear, she tried to break free from his penetration. Gently pulling out from her the count spoke calmly.

"It is done, you will in time become a real lady of the night, enjoy this gift and take care of my son."

Turning rapidly Melinda looked at the Count and asked,

"What the fuck are you going on about? I have not forgotten you owe me £500 mate."

The count, slowly putting his clothes back on did not answer nor give Melinda eye contact. Fully dressed, his face stern, his posture military like, he turned and left the room.

Chapter Six

Now the weekend, Tony had worked hard to assemble the beds, arrange the other furniture and get the manor in a liveable condition. He could not help feeling like 'Vamps Bitch' as he felt the desire to order more cushions for the new three piece suite.

'I am gonna relax today, no matter what.' He thought pulling a small lever on the side of the sofa, which extended the recliner to an almost bed like position. Holding his multi control remote, he pressed the buttons in the correct sequence to turn on the Digi box, TV & surround sound processor,

"Ahh, this isn't so bad." As he stopped surfing and locked onto the sports channel. Although the football was the game he wanted to watch, he took his eyes off the TV and nervously looked right to left. Without looking over his shoulder he said,

"Vamp is that you?" as he felt a cold chill on the back of his neck.

"Morning Tony, you are at last learning to trust your feelings. You promised you would explain what all this fancy stuff is."

"Yeah, I did old boy, have a seat and I will run you through it."

Explaining blow by blow what each shiny silver box did the Count could not help feel very tired, it was not often he needed to learn and absorb new information at such a pace.

"You humans have been busy whilst I've been hibernating."

Although the Count was taking his time to understand what the technology in front of him could do for him, he shouted,

"Pass the ball!"

Tony surprised by this reaction, couldn't help think,

'Vamp you're not so bad, fair call, pass the ball you moron!'

Feeling the excitement of the game, Tony stood and ventured off into the kitchen. He returned armed with two large cold bottles of beer and a bowl of crisps. Not really thinking he handed the Count one of the bottles, as he set the bowl down on the table. After a short while, Tony gave the Count a stern stare, to say take the bottle.

"Tony, I believe you are forgetting something?"

"Cripes, what's wrong with me, forgot where I was for a second. Can you not drink anything else then?"

"No Tony, all I can consume is blood."

"Where are you stashing your emergency supplies then, I may have an idea you may like."

The Count had no real reason not to trust Tony, so told him where it was hidden.

"I'll be a sec." Tony said as he shot off in the direction of the hidden blood bank. Tony was gone for about ten minutes, when he returned with a boyish cheeky grin.

"See how you get on with this then." Handing the Count a cup of blood, fresh from the microwave.

Smelling the contents of the cup before it came into sight, the Count smiled. Sipping the warm/hot blood, Tony excitedly asked.

"How's that, is it too hot? I gave it 30 seconds in the Mic, never done blood before so not sure, I certainly wasn't going to test it for you."

The Count pleased with Tony's efforts replied,

"A little hotter than I prefer but a vast improvement on cold, thank you."

Feeling a bond forming, Tony slipped into the idea of the Vamp being his buddy.

"We have really got to sort your dress sense out mate. If you are going to be hanging out with me, you are going to need a new wardrobe."

"Excellent, you understand your purpose here, I require for you to protect me from humans. I need for you to teach me to talk like you, I need to be able to mingle and not stand out in a crowd. Do you think you can help me with this Tony?"

Tony suddenly remembering his place, burst out with,

"We need to go shopping, I'll make you look the 'Muts Nuts.' Oh my god I am a woman!"

Laughing quietly, the Count thought 'I do like Tony' and also felt a friendship forming.

Tony lifted his arm to look at his watch, which proved quite difficult, as he was holding six shopping bags in each hand. Briefly shaking as he fought the weight, he held his arm steady to focus on his watch. He noted it was nearly 6pm.

"We better call it a day old boy, the shops will be shut soon."

"Yes Tony, I require to return to the house and change clothes."

"Well you are not short of clothes now, I think we have bought the shops out, my feet are killing me."

Loading the shopping bags into the back of his Grand Voyager, Tony frantically positioned them so that they would not move in transit. The Count sat patiently, monitoring his servant's movements but not forth coming with any help. Twisting the ignition key Tony said,

"Belt up, don't want you flying through the screen unnecessarily."

The Count turned his head slowly towards Tony,

"It would not cause me a problem, you forget I am immortal."

"Na, Boss I haven't forgotten but you told me to protect you, the last thing I want is the fuzz pulling us and drawing unnecessary attention."

"What is the fuzz, Tony?"

"Sorry, the police."

"A very good point, I will belt up, as you put it. And how do I do that?"

Leaning over the Count Tony grabbed the seatbelt. Pulling it across the Count he stopped and handed the buckle to him.

"That shiny bit goes in that black thing next to the seat, the bit with the red button on it. I am amazed you can work out where someone is and pop out of thin air next to them but you can't work out a seatbelt!"

The Count not fazed by Tony's sarcasm calmly spoke,

"You should have seen me when I was first getting the hang of the teleporting."

Tony laughed loudly, as he understood the Count was trying to be funny and relax his image.

Checking his interior mirror, Tony noticed the van behind him was driving extremely close and had been for the last ten minutes of the journey.

"Get off my arse, twat head!" Tony yelled, still looking in the mirror.

The driver of the white van looked at Tony via the mirror aggressively and shortened the gap between the vehicles further still. Tony now at boiling point slammed on the brakes just long enough, to make the van nearly go into the back of him. Thinking the van driver would get the idea and back off; Tony was surprised that the driver accelerated hard swerving erratically to allow the van to pull alongside the car.

Putting his foot hard down on the accelerator the 4.2 litre people carrier slowly responded. The auto box took its time to find the right gear but it was too late the van had overtaken and cut Tony up. With the van barely stopping, the driver rushed out and stood in the middle of the street, gesturing to Tony that he wanted to talk man to man.

Stopping the car Tony looked at the Count and said,

"I won't be long just finding out what this nutters problem is."

Walking towards the van driver Tony looked confident but not confrontational.

"You got a problem pal?"

The man said nothing and advanced towards Tony. As he entered range of Tony the driver reached back fist closed, launching an almighty swing. Connecting with Tony's chin, the blow strong enough to floor a rhino made a cracking sound, as his fist engaged with Tony's jaw. Tony's head jolted in the direction of the punch, a large droplet of saliva overtook his face, as Tony let out a loud cry.

His head now moving at a speed his body could not do anything else but follow. Tony reached out with both hands to break his fall and enable him to get back up quickly. Tumbling over several times, Tony stood straight back up. Shaking his head as if to try and wake himself up he rubbed his jaw line where the fist had impacted. He realised he was not hurt nor effected by the mighty blow.

Astonished, Tony was still standing, the man ran towards him, launching a bombardment of blows. An uppercut to Tony's stomach actually lifted him clean off his feet. Keeping direct eye contact Tony said,

"Is that the best you've got?"

As the man lowered his guard in sheer amazement, the Counts figure appeared behind Tony. Without warning the Count launched his open hand into the man's chest. The force generated would easily fold a car clean in half. The man shot backward rising about three feet in the air. His arms held in front of him with his legs perpendicular to his arms. His hair flowed in front of his head in the velocity of his travel. His zero to sixty mph in 0.5 of a second journey was brought to abrupt end, as he crashed through the back doors of his van.

The Count, who appeared to be protective towards Tony, marched towards the van. His stride, long and powerful, with vigour an oncoming locomotive would not be able to stop.

The man looked at the Count, limp with life understanding his internal organs were severely crushed.

"What the fuck are you?" Spitting blood as he spoke.

"Your worst nightmare." The Count boldly explained, as his face turned from a well groomed man, to a fang bearing demon.

His fingers arched in a cat paw manner he thrust them into the man's right chest. Letting off an immensely loud cry the man looked at the counts bloody hand, his facial expression one of terror and confusion, as he watched his heart beat its final few beats in the counts palm. Lifting his top lip only in its left corner, the Count growled exposing his large fangs. The man empty of life, eyes flickered into the back of their sockets, as he collapsed into a heap.

"What is wrong with you?" Tony demanded, "I had it covered."

Taking a deep breath the Counts eyes widened as he metamorphosed back to his charming human form.

"I will not tolerate human inferior behaviour."

"Note to self, don't piss him off." Tony muttered.

"What do we do with his van and body now?"

The Count paused and explained,

"I am sure a man of your intelligence; you don't believe everything you see on the news. It is not always as it seems."

Extending his right arm the Count held his hand in front of him, his palm open but firm. Several seconds passed, before the van spontaneously burst into flames, engulfing the man's body.

"Should have got that dodgy fuel line fixed, this is the trouble with old vans." the count said under his breath.

Tony could not help but think of the image of Richard on the news and agreed with the count, things are definitely not always as they seem.

The count broke his thought,

"Tony you are coming out with me tonight, I must continue with my work."

Clever enough not to disobey, Tony replied,

"Whatever you say Boss, What are we up to?"

"You will see my friend."

CHAPTER SEVEN

It had been two days since Melinda's encounter with the Count. She sat in her one bed flat, vacantly staring at the TV, the room dark, only lit by the natural light from outside. Wearing just her knickers and her bra, she couldn't understand why she was still feeling so hot. Wiping a bead of sweat from her forehead, she swung her legs over the armchair, turning her head to look over her shoulder to watch the TV. As she looked at the small portable TV, the picture seemed to go out of focus and become very fuzzy for a brief second and then slowly refocus.

Licking her lips she acknowledged she was very thirsty but found it strange she did not crave water. Licking her lips one more time, she moved her tongue across her front teeth. Pausing for a second, she repeated the exercise and focused her tongue's attention on her K9 region. Feeling an abnormally sharp pointed K9, she tried to recall the last time she checked her teeth. Paying no further attention, she gently closed her eyes in hope that this would ease her pounding headache.

Braving to open her eyes she looked at her hands. She noticed that they were shaking quite vigorously. Her combined symptoms did not really worry her, as she had experienced many a bad withdrawal before. The only real difference was she did not feel the urge to tear the flat apart to find a fix.

"I feel like crap." she softly spoke under her breath thinking if she would be able to work later that night. Closing her eyes again she heard a distant voice in the middle of her head say,

"Don't fight it Melinda, it won't be long, soon you will feel invincible."

For a moment her headache cleared. As it did a clear mental picture of the Count filled her mind.

Startled by this image, she sat bolt upright from her slumped couch potato like posture.

Taking in a large gulp of air, her face became stricken with fear, as she worked out that this was no bad come down.

After taking a long cool shower, Melinda had managed to calm her excessive sweating. Wearing a mini skirt, thigh length boots and a cropped vest, she stood in her usual place on Vauxhall Street. Looking at her watch she acknowledged that most bars would be chucking people out and prepared her posture ready for the next kerb crawler. Watching the body language of the oncoming cars, she could normally correctly guess which cars would stop. A Porsche Boxster showed the tell tell signs, Melinda waited patiently. As the car slowed to a standstill, the driver lowered the passenger window and lent across the passenger's seat.

"How much to suck me plums?"

Whilst Melinda thought of her answer, she also thought,

'Why is it always the rich ones who feel it necessary to be rude and make her feel like scum?'

"For you sweetheart, only £50.00."

"Sounds like a deal, hop in."

Lowering herself into the sports car, the man took his time to look her long legs up and down. Hoping for a sneak preview of her knickers, as her skirt hitched up slightly.

Giving the man a stern look he broke from his perverting and realised Melinda wanted cash up front.

"Sorry, how rude of me, here you go fifty as agreed."

Taking the money with no real reaction to the man, she said,

"Take the next left; I'll give you directions to a good spot, where we will not be disturbed."

"Direction honey, I want erection!" the man joked in a condescending voice.

Driving for no more than 5 minutes the man parked up into a back street as instructed.

Switching off the engine, the man pulled his seat handle to move his seat back to its furthest position. Being a sports car this was not far but provided enough clearance between the steering wheel and the man's body for Melinda's head.

Keen to get his monies worth the man unfastened his zip and released his belt and trouser button.

"All yours girl, do your magic. I want to cum over your face by the way, is that all included in the price?"

Ignoring the man's question, Melinda gently leant towards the man taking his manhood in her hand. Using long strokes she manoeuvred her hand up and down his penis, readying it for oral pleasure. Lowering her head into his crotch, she opened her mouth and took his impressive cock in. Due to the size of him she was not sure if she would be able to perform her usual party trick of engulfing the entire shaft and licking his balls. Whilst she plucked up the courage, she bobbed her mouth up and down taking about ¾ of his shaft in. The man sat back hard into his seat, shutting his eyes he pushed his head back into the headrest, smiling cheekily as he enjoyed her talents.

"Oh you are good, you've done this before haven't you?"

Melinda thought,

'Why do men always ask silly questions when you have a big cock in your mouth? One, I'm not going to answer with a mouthful and two if you piss me off I might just bite your cock off.'

As she thought this, a strange sensation came over her. She suddenly felt very much alive and her sense of smell seemed to be 500 times more acute. As she sucked his shaft from top to bottom she thought she could physically hear his heart beating in his erect penis. A sensation similar to her needing a fix and finding a bag of cocaine overwhelmed her. Her instincts and behaviour became very much animal like, her rhythm on the man's penis increasing dramatically.

"Hey Hey, calm down tiger, I don't want to cum too quickly and as I said I want to shoot my load all over your face."

Without any command from Melinda, her previously sensitive K9's grew to form two- inch long fangs. Taking her head away from the man's penis briefly she located his main vein running up his shaft. Her pupil's now glowing white, providing her with night vision, locked target on the pulsing vein.

Thrusting her head quickly downwards she bit into his stem, sinking her long fangs into his main vein.

"Ahhhhh! What the fuck are you doing?" the man screamed trying to shake her off his manhood in panic.

Melinda fed hard and quick, sucking litres of blood per second. The man grabbing Melinda by the ears tried frantically to pull her off his genitals.

"Ahhhhhhhhhhh!" he shouted at the top of his voice.

Melinda nested her head deeper into the man's lap, thrashing erratically, similar to a crocodile.

The man's mouth formally shrieking with pain slowly dropped. His eyes failing to respond became still, as Melinda sucked the last bit of life from his body.

Rising from her feed, she remembered the telepathic message from the Count. She agreed, she did feel invincible and understood her purpose in the food chain.

Nervously, Tony sat next to the Count in a trendy bar. Not being a school night the bar was busy.

"Why do you look so on edge, Tony?"

Taking his time to think before answering, he said,

"Well I don't mean to be rude but the last time I went to a bar looking for talent, I ended getting your finger in my neck. Kinda worried what will happen to me tonight!"

"Tony you need to understand, you need not fear me. If you do as I ask, I think you will enjoy your new future."

Taking a big swig of his pint, Tony looked around the bar. He was quite pleased to view that there was a fair amount of good looking women occupying the venue.

"Which one do you fancy Tony?" the Count softly enquired.

"Er, it's hard to say, there are so many fit babes in here!"

The count remained quiet and methodically rubbed his chin. After a couple of hours passed, the Count broke his silence,

"What about that one over there? The blonde with a dolphin tattoo on her left shoulder."

Tony looked around the busy bar, searching as if he had lost a child at a shopping centre.

"Oh yes, she is hot!" he remarked, as he locked eyes on the stunning young lady.

"Her mate is nasty too!"

"I take it you mean she is pretty as well?" the Count confirmed.

"Not many Benny."

Feeling like the conversation was going nowhere the Count said,

"Those two, it shall be then."

Tony afraid to ask remained quiet.

"Barman, would you be so kind as to take over a bottle of your finest Champagne to those two lovely ladies, compliments of me of course."

The Count watched attentively as the barman took the bottle to their table. As the barman placed the Champagne on the table, he gestured towards the Count, as he explained to the ladies who had bought it.

Replying with a warm infectious smile, the Count acknowledged their thanks.

"Do you think that buying them a bottle of bubbly; will guarantee getting into their knickers? I've got news for you Vamps; they can probably drink that in under ten minutes and will be onto the next guy."

"Tony, I am sure the night will go our way. I am allowed to have a little fun aren't I?"

"You're the Boss!!"

The Count left it about twenty minutes before rising from his seat and gliding over to the ladies table. Sitting down beside the lady without the tattoo he said,

"Ladies, excuse me. Women as fine as you two deserve nothing but the best. Please accept this bottle with the gesture it is intended. "

Although a very cheesy line, which most ladies would shoot the man down with several choice words, one of the ladies replied,

"Wow, handsome, charming and rich. Aren't we the lucky ones? "

It had nothing to do with the fact she was gazing into the Counts mesmerising stare.

"Please join us."

"Only if you insist!"

The Count looked over to Tony to indicate the coast was clear and to come over to the table.

"Ladies, this is Tony a very good friend of mine."

Not having the same magnetising effect, Tony greeted the ladies,

"How you doing!!!"

Not responding, the ladies shuffled round the table to make space for Tony.

"So what are your names then?" Tony asked.

The lady with the tattoo answered

"This is Shirley and I'm Rihanna."

After several drinks later and lots of polite banter Shirley and Rihanna excused themselves to the ladies toilets. They wanted to discuss away from Tony and the Count, who they wished to pair up with.

Returning several minutes later with their makeup freshly reapplied, Shirley asked,

"Shall we hit a club or something?"

The Count paused briefly before answering,

"I like the sound of the something; shall we carry on the party at my mansion?"

Giggling like little schoolgirls they both agreed this was what they had in mind.

Travelling back to the manor, the Count sat behind Tony, the girls sat in the back row of the seven seat people carrier. Although the girls both had intentions of riding the arses off Tony and the Count, the girls wished to keep their distance. It suddenly dawned on Rihanna, that they did not know the Count's name, she asked in quite an abrupt voice,

"You have not even told us your name. I thought you were the one with all the manners?"

"Sorry my sweet, how rude of me because of your beauty I wanted to know as much about you, not boring old me. I forgot to ask what music are you into, Tony has just installed the state of the art sound system."

"R&B and Happy House is the mainstream of my music." Rihanna replied not noticing that the Count had again not answered her question.

Shirley not wanting to be left out of the conversation asked,

"So, is he your chauffeur then?"

"Who, Tony? No he is a good companion."

"Yeah right, so what do you do for a living to afford a chauffeur?"

"I am head of a global pest control organisation, I do ok." The Count replied.

The girl's questions were silenced as they arrived at the gates to the manor. Clicking the remote from the inside of the car the gates slowly opened.

As they approached the Manor, Rihanna exclaimed,

"I bet this place cost a few quid." Although she was actually thinking it looked a bit creepy.

"It was cheaper than you may think, Rihanna. Right place at the right time scenario shall we say."

Tony switched the ignition off, bringing the purr of the gas-guzzler to a standstill. Frantically unfastening his seatbelt and exiting the car, Tony made his way to the Counts door, opening it on his behalf.

"Thank you, Tony." The count spoke in a calm smooth voice, as he slowly left the car. The girls looked at each other and broke into a brief fit of laughter, they were confident that their new men would be a lucrative opportunity.

Both Rihanna and Shirley were very attractive ladies and knew how to string men along. They knew that if they gave Tony and the Count what they wanted, they would be able to milk these guys for thousands.

Tony also held the door open for Rihanna and Shirley, being a gentleman he diverted his eyes as they negotiated themselves from their seats. Both their skirts were very short and did not leave much to the imagination. Rihanna positioned herself and lowered one long leg to establish a footing. Tony couldn't help but look, starting at her black stiletto; he went upwards over every millimetre, along the contour of her perfectly formed smooth leg. He thought to himself,

'I bet you would get a dry old tongue, licking those legs all the way to the top!'

As Rihanna gently brushed by Tony, she paused and caressed his cheek with her hand. Tony pleased with this affection; his thoughts were suddenly interrupted, as she planted a sweet moist kiss on the same cheek.

"Thank you, Tony" she said in a cheeky schoolgirl voice.

"You're welcome." He replied, quietly grinning to himself.

Expecting the same gesture from Shirley, he found a little disappointment as she got out of the car and made straight for the manor door.

"No, Thank You, frigid bitch." Tony muttered under his breath. He thought,

'Maybe, I am in with a chance with Rihanna then'

This new thought excited him and he quickly followed the girls into the manor.

Loading R&B Anthems 2006 into the CD player, the Count looked uneasy. His fingernails yet again were proving to be a problem. It had taken him the entire time before the girls entered the room to actually get the disc out of its case.

The sensual beat of R Kelly filled the room. Tony a bit of mover, moon walked over to Rihanna and asked,

"What can I get you fine ladies to drink?"

"Champers darling!" Rihanna replied.

Tony was about to shout 'Vamps" when he quickly realised that he could not and quickly changed it to.

"Roberto, do you have a sec over here?"

The count turned to Tony with a glum expression, then quickly understood Tony's behaviour

"Of course Tony, be right with you."

Rihanna looked at Shirley and spoke with amazement,

"Ahh, Roberto's his name. You gonna get some Roberto!"

The Count met with Tony in the Kitchen,

"What is the problem Tony?"

"Well Boss, you said to protect you and allow you to mingle and stuff. Well those finger nails are really not helping; can you not give them a trim?"

"Tony, I would really like to reduce their length but I have yet found anything that can cut them."

"Remind me in the morning or when you surface. I think I know what will do the trick. Anyway I get the impression that Rihanna's up for me, so do you mind if I give it a go?"

"Tony, I think any of these two ladies is a result, go on fill ya boots!!"

Tony laughed infectiously as they walked back into the entertainments room. He found it very funny how the Count was trying to talk slang with a mix of old fashion posh talk. He thought to himself,

'I call that Slangish.'

"Ladies, your champers!"

Both Rihanna and Shirley took their glasses and took a healthy swig.

Although they were both well lubricated, the extra charge of alcohol was needed to settle their nerves.

Not sure what to do next, Tony sat crossing his legs as he took a healthy sized swig of his champagne. The Count following Tony's lead also sat but he sat with such a confidence, it was obvious that he was the Master of the manor.

Looking Rihanna up and down, Tony thought,

'Wow, you are delightful, this new life is not turning out to bad!"

Rihanna noticed Tony's affectionate stare and broke away from her conversation with Shirley. Walking slowly, almost in slow motion, her hair bouncing with every step, she moved towards Tony, finally settling on his knee.

Gliding her fingernail over his cheek, she looked him direct in the eyes with a seductive glare and asked,

"Do you want to fool around?"

Without a seconds delay, Tony responded,

"Yeap, Yes please, I mean that will be nice, what with me, you sure?"

Rihanna smiled, as she found his innocence quite a turn on and lent forward to engage in a romantic kiss.

Watching Tony & Rihanna getting it on, Shirley understood she needed to follow suit.

"Do you like what you see?"

She asked the Count.

In a confident smooth voice he replied,

"What I see is magical; shall we adjourn to the bedroom?"

Not fazed by his forward approach, she kindly accepted his invitation and met him for a passionate kiss, as he rose from his chair.

Tony really overpowered by Rihanna's beauty, felt quite nervous as if he was about to lose his virginity. He lay on the bed, motionless in a star like position wearing only his white y-front pants. Rihanna stood at the end of the bed and looked at Tony with a seductive glint in her eye. Unfastening her blouse she bared her plump firm breasts, held firmly in place by a push up bra. Still wearing her skirt, high heels and bra she advanced towards Tony. Placing gently affectionate kisses on his body, as she headed towards Tony's mouth. Teasing him she paused before embracing him with a passionate deep kiss. Tony relaxed as he enjoyed the kiss; he heard rhythmic moans coming from the wall behind his headboard. It was clear that the Count was already doing the wild thing and it sounded as if Shirley was definitely enjoying it. The muffled cry came from the other side of the wall,

"Oh my god I am coming, yes, yes, yes, yeeeeesss!"

Rihanna rather turned on by her friends cry delved into Tony's pants, massaging his penis to a full erection.

Hopping off, she frantically unfastened her skirt, kicking it to the floor as it got hooked on one of her high heels. Striding Tony she inserted his manhood, groaning with satisfaction as she did, she gently formed a safe rhythm.

Rihanna, bit her bottom lip slightly, as she felt his manhood go deep inside her. She looked down at Tony and noticed he did not look as if he was enjoying it as much as she was, when Tony twitched erratically. Rihanna felt his warm cum enter her as well as his manhood quickly reduce in size and become limp.

"Sorry you're so hot, I couldn't control it. Give me a few minutes and I'll be good to go again."

Frustrated by the poor show, she moodily got off Tony.

"Don't worry I am tired anyway!" she said in a comforting voice, whilst she repositioned her knickers.

Rihanna had not been lying next to Tony for long when his snoring smothered the epic session that was still going on in the next room. Rihanna lay still, looking at the ceiling for about another hour, before she thought

'I had a 50/50 chance of getting the stud muffin and I got it wrong. Hurry up Shirley I want to get out of here!'

With Tony snoring like a bear, she thought 'what have I got to lose.' Placing her hand inside her knickers, she started to pleasure herself.

The Count thrust hard into Shirley from behind, they had just changed from 'Doggy' position to both standing. The Count held one breast with one hand and with the other clenched her throat tightly.

"Now for the orgasm of your life." He said in a dark voice.

Lowering his mouth to her neck, his long fangs extended, sinking them into her neck Shirley let off a loud cry. Shirley tried to struggle but her fate was inevitable, the Count maintained his rhythm as he slowly drank her blood. Thrusting his penis harder still, the Count released his thick warm cum inside her. Her body tingling with many sensations surprised Shirley, as she also climaxed.

Rihanna who was listening to the noisy performance needed little motion of her finger, before she was crying in ecstasy herself.

The Count removed his fangs and not fully fed, he said,

"Look after my child; I will always be here for you."

Exhausted from the whole experience Shirley felt the urge to faint. The Count removed himself from her and lowered her gently to the bed.

"Sleep well my sweet, sleep well."

Chapter Eight

Tony had been a very long time dropping the girls back. Unusually the Count had surfaced and was surprised Tony was not there waiting for his next instruction. Content with the progress of his master plan the Count decided to take the time to try and operate the TV. The Count a demon of vast intelligence rarely had to be shown anything twice and found the operation of TV, Digi box and surround sound quite easy, well except for his nails getting in the way.

As Tony had, the Count repeatedly pressed the channel up button, until he stopped on a channel, which looked like it might interest him. He had found the Comedy channel; full of American sit-coms he thought that this would improve his slang. Quite mesmerised the Count was not aware that a further hour had passed.

"Morning!" Tony yelled as he marched in through the front door.

"Have I got a surprise for you, me old mucker!"

For the first time in his existence, the Count felt somewhat worried and wondered what Tony was up to.

"Dare I ask?" the count enquired as he made his way into the lobby where Tony was.

"Here you go. If this doesn't do it, we are screwed." Tony bragged, waving an industrial professional series disc cutter in the air.

"Come on; time to trim those nails of yours!"

"What is that Tony?"

"This mate is the Rolls Royce, the mother of all nail clippers. It's called a disc cutter, capable of cutting straight through a car door, so we should be able to take those talons down a peg or two. Come on step outside to my salon."

"Are you totally mad, Tony?"

"What you're not chicken are you?"

The Count considered his odds and almost burst out with a plucking sound, but thought I must trust Tony.

Now in the garden, the count nervously held both his hands in front of him. The weather for late April was surprisingly sunny; the Count had not burst into flames yet so Tony thought all the other stuff about vampires must be true.

Pressing the trigger, the 8inch blade sprung into life, spinning at over 5,200 rpm.

"Ready?" Tony asked.

"I suppose so!"

Tony moved the spinning cutting blade towards the Counts index finger, pausing just before contact. Engaging the blade with the counts nail, a piercing grinding sound filled the air. Amber sparks shot off the spinning disc as the nail slowly reduced in length.

"Yes! Thought this would work."

A smile came to the Count's face, this was the first time anyone had actually done something nice for him.

He was also delighted to see his nails diminish before his very eyes.

"Well done Tony, you are a star."

As the cutting wheel slowly came to a halt, the Count took a minute to admire his smart new ten digits.

"Tony this means a lot to me, I shall reward you dearly for this."

"Ah shut up, you would have done the same for me?"

"Why of course, I would." The count replied as they strolled back to the manor.

"Back to business, last night went quite well I believe. The only issue I have is I require to perform this three times a night.

"You dirty dog!" Tony joked.

"No Tony, the incubation period of my children is only three months. I require to heavily populate my children amongst humans. Their infancy is short as well is their childhood, within two years they will be fully-grown and of adult form. As you can see I have much work to do and very little time."

"You make it sound so tough. So basically your job is to shag all the time. The real downer is that you only pick the hot ones, no scanks. Mate most men would die for a job like that."

"They have, Tony, they have." The count replied in a knowing voice.

Back in front of the TV, Tony asked,

"So what do you want me to do whilst you are getting your freak on?"

"Most women do not venture out alone, so my friend you will require to entertain the other lady(s). However you see fit!"

Tony was just about to answer, when he paused to listen to the TV news.

"A fifth person has been found dead in the Vauxhall area. It is suspected that all five victims have been murdered by the same killer. It is alleged that this serial killer may be a woman, pretending to be a lady of the night. Police have issued a warning and urge men to take great caution if tempted to hire a prostitute"

As the presenter took a breath before reading the next story, the Count uttered,

"Melinda you are feeding well."

Tony looked at the Count with a vacant stare. Although he had no choice of his involvement, he was unsure if he really wanted to be part of it any longer.

Melinda woke about 2pm, exhausted from her previous night's activities. Prior to her new gift, she would take several minutes to stir. Instead her eyes opened from sealed shut to wide open. Taking just a few seconds to work out where she was, she threw the sheets off the bed and rose fresh and vibrant. Delighted with her new lease of life she felt fulfilled and cleansed. She thought to herself,

'People pay a lot of money to go to health spas and stuff, all they need to do is be turned into a vampire. I feel fucking fantastic!'

With a skip in her stride she made her way to the shower. As she massaged lather over the curves of body she felt a bit sexy. The only problem with her new nightly activities was, she was killing her clients before satisfying herself. Cupping her left breast she gently caressed it, flicking her nipples in the way she liked it. With the other hand she slowly rotated her finger on and around her clit. Closing her eyes she gently bit her bottom lip, as she brought herself to climax. She slightly shuddered as she enjoyed the sensations of her orgasm. She paused for a second before she reached for the shower cream and applied it to her vagina.

As Melinda walked in to the bedroom, she remembered that she was about a week late from having her period. She wondered if it was because of her now being a vampire or if she was actually pregnant. Standing side profile to her full-length mirror she saw the answer to her question. Her stomach was bloated more than her usual 'ON' stomach, about double in size.

"Oh shit. I cannot believe that this is going to be a good thing." Melinda uttered.

Quickly spinning round, she looked at her reflection from her other side, thinking for some reason the bump may look smaller. As she focused hard on the contours of her increasing bulge, she noticed a slight movement from within.

"What the? No way it can't be that big already?"

Confused she immediately began to worry; her head became swamped with questions. 'I hope that this is not going to affect business?'

'How big will it get?'
'Will it feed on milk or blood?'
'Will it look human?'

'Will it?'

Her thoughts were interrupted by the Counts voice, his voice rang loud and strong in her mind, she could do nothing else but listen.

"Melinda, I understand your many questions. Trust me all will be ok in two more months you will give birth to a beautiful boy, he will feed as you do, he will develop quickly and will no longer depend upon you. You will have many more babies all beautiful, as all my family are."

As his voice and image faded from her mind, Melinda frowned and said,

"Many more babies? I don't like the sound of that bit."

Melinda decided she was not going to think anymore about what was cooking in her tummy but instead treat herself to some retail therapy.

Dressed in tight black leggings, red high heels and a white low cut vest, she tipped the taxi driver generously.

"Thanks sweetheart." said the taxi driver just as Melinda closed the door of the taxi. Melinda spent the next hour trying on various tops; she tried a pair of hipsters that left nothing much to the imagination. She loved Harrods and knew the best departments and their layout like the back of her hand. As she strolled from department to department she couldn't help notice that a man in his late thirties seemed to be following her. Making note of his location she upped her pace and ventured back out onto the busy street.

Without making it obvious she occasionally glanced over her shoulder to see if he was following. This type of behaviour was not uncommon for Melinda, as being a stunner she often got weird and extra attention from men. Looking over her right shoulder she saw that her stalker was in pursuit. Deciding to have a little fun, she picked up her stroll to an almost jog. Not checking if he was keeping up or even still following, she ducked down a small alley between two retail outlets. Facing in the direction of the opening she stood legs wide and waited patiently. Within a minute the man now also almost jogging turned into the alley way, not looking up he advanced down the narrow passage. Looking up to check on her whereabouts, he came to an abrupt holt as she stood boldly in front of him. Jolting his head back slightly as he came to a standstill his face turned to an expression of fright. Melinda had not changed her appearance; the man was frightened as he had been rumbled.

"Want some of this buddy?" Melinda asked in a provocative voice, whilst grasping her crotch.

The man intimidated by her aggressive action looked nervously over his shoulder with a view for a hasty retreat.

"Come on this one is on the house!" Melinda taunted.

The man now knowing she was a professional, suddenly found the courage to advance forward his thoughts now very ugly towards her.

"Oh yes baby, you gonna get yourself some." As he got within a foot of Melinda she looked him directly in the eyes, her eyes blinked pure white and became very cat like.

Noticing her abnormal stare the man knew something was not right and turned to run. Before he could gain any distance Melinda leapt forward with vigour, fangs fully extended. As she advanced through the air she let off a piercing hiss opening her mouth wide ready for impact. Landing on target she sank her fangs deep into his neck, wriggling slightly to ensure a good bite. Putting her hand over his mouth to capture his cry for help, she forced him backwards and up against the wall. Feeding hard and fast the man paralysed as he stood, wondering when and if it would end. Gulping hard, the man started to feel very weak and dizzy; moments later he was no longer.

Releasing her bite and grip she let him fall effortlessly to the ground, as he slumped into a heap she said.

"Feeding for two now, nothing personal honest."

Nearly two months had passed; Melinda was hugely pregnant and almost ready to drop. Although she looked a similar shape to a space hopper, she had managed to keep her business going and was feeding sometimes three times a night. She did find it strange that there was quite a big following for having sex with pregnant woman. Well this cult was being diminished on a nightly basis.

Sitting in her flat, she held her stomach with both hands and moved the hardened stomach in a circular motion.

"Ooh, utt-oh." She moaned, as she felt the sensation alter and watched a trickle of water form a pool around her feet.

Rushing downstairs with no overnight bag she flagged a passing Taxi.

"Hospital please, I'm having a baby."

The taxi driver remained calm and sped towards the hospital. Arriving at the hospital the taxi driver leapt out and helped Melinda to the reception. Fumbling in her handbag she pulled out a twenty pound note,

"Here thank you."

"No darling, this one is on me. Good luck with the baby, God Bless you."

The midwife checked Melinda's vitals and agreed she was soon going to have a baby.

Slightly put off by the stirrups, Melinda tried to get comfortable, knowing she had a lot of work to do.

"Push, Push!" the midwife chanted.

The pain of the 15lb boy working his way down her birth canal caused Melinda concern. In addition to the ordeal of the birth, she was also fighting not changing in front of the midwife. The pain sensations triggered her natural defence mechanism, as she screamed and pushed her eyes glowed white, yellow and then back to her stunning clear blue. Hoping that the midwife had not seen this she focused hard willing her fangs not to extend.

"One more push, Melinda, one more long hard push."

Melinda took a deep breath, clenched the bed sheet and screamed,

"Arrrggggghhhhhh"

Her cry was silenced, by the sound of her baby boy catching his first breath at the top of his lungs.

Cutting the cord and cleaning the baby the midwife handed the boy to Melinda to perform skin on skin.

"Do you have a name for him?"

Not answering, Melinda suddenly thought,

'I haven't even thought that far, gosh what shall I call him?' The short thirty minute delivery had not really given her any time to prepare in any shape of form.

"Leon, he looks like a Leon to me, I thought I would name him once I've seen the little blighter."

"What a lovely name, I will enter it onto your records."

Moving Melinda to the maternity ward Melinda asked,

"When can I leave?"

"Once we have seen the baby is latching on ok and you are rested, you could be ok to leave, say tomorrow?"

Melinda's face, which should have been delighted, frowned as she wondered if she could go a night without feeding.

"I'll leave you now to get some rest."

The midwife pulled the curtains around Melinda's bed and left.

Looking down at her new baby boy, Melinda smiled and thought,

'The Count was right, he is beautiful and perfectly formed.' She realised like lots of other new mums she was forming a bond.

Little Leon twitched and stirred as a natural reaction to being hungry. Wriggling in Melinda's arms she knew what she had to do. Bearing one breast she offered her nipple to Leon. In the usual manner she tempted his lips with her nipple and waited for him to open his mouth and lock on. Leon made a little grunting noise, as he smelt his mums scent. Opening his little mouth Melinda moved him onto her nipple,

"Jesus, Mother of God." She cried, as Leon's little fangs sank either side of her.

Making a slight sucking sound Leon was content and continued to feed on Melinda's blood for a good ten minutes.

Literally with another mouth to feed, Melinda knew she would not be able to stay the night. Self sufficient in her feeding she quietly got dressed and left the hospital.

Back at her flat she organised the cot and other baby products, she had just purchased in a fashion that would provide Leon with the warmth and comfort he needed. Changing his nappy and allowing him to feed one more time, she said,

"Hey little man, I've got to pop out and get us dinner, I will not be long. Sleep little man, I will be back by the time you next need to feed."

Double locking the door of her flat behind her, she ventured off to the nearest bar.

She had only been sat at the bar for ten minutes, when a young man in his mid twenties sat on the bar stool next to her.

"Can I get you a drink?" he nervously asked.

"I am very thirsty, but there is nothing here I really fancy. Save your money and forget the polite chit chat. You want to get naughty with me don't you?"

A little bit taken aback with her answer he paused to collate his thoughts and answered,

"Well yes honey, do you want to get a room?"

"I'm feeling rather horny, why wait? Let's do it in the toilet!"

Taking his hand, she led him towards the ladies. She walked with a wide stride and appeared to be in a hurry. The man not so sure about toilet sex held back slightly and looked as if he was being towed by Melinda.

Locking the cubical door, the man looked at Melinda to ascertain where they were going to start. With him now trapped, she moved in for the kill, gently kissing his neck, her fangs extended down. Using her tongue she ran it up and down his neck. The man not believing his luck grabbed one of her breasts and massaged it, like he was making bread.

Sinking her fangs into his jugular she drank hard, the man squinting as the pain overwhelmed his body. Reacting to the pain he squeezed Melinda's breast hard in an attempt of hurting her to make her stop. This was pointless as Melinda was not letting go for anyone and rather liked rough action. The man, open mouthed couldn't understand why he could not move,

'Why don't I just throw her off me, I must be stronger than her.' As his thoughts faded, his heart had stopped and he was fully drained of blood. The final sensation of pins & needles all over his body was the last thing he felt.

Removing her bite from his neck, she slowly ran her tongue over her fangs, ensuring every little last drop of blood was consumed.

Returning to her flat she opened the door, pleased to hear Leon was quiet.

"Holly Crap. You startled me!" She remarked, noticing the Count standing over the crib.

"He is magnificent, isn't he?"

"He's a hungry little critter; I know that much for nothing."

"Feed him and then we can begin."

"Begin What?"

"You are now able to bear more of my children, valuable time I cannot waste. I must impregnate you now."

Melinda not even knowing the man's name who stood before her said,

"Firstly, can I at least know your name and secondly I gave birth this morning, give me a break."

"Melinda, this is not your decision to make, my name is Roberto, now feed Leon I have much to do." The count changed his subtle tone of voice to a commanding growl.

Putting Leon down full and content, she looked at the Count with a slight tear in her eye. She knew it was pointless to resist but she was really sore from childbirth.

Timidly she bent over and braced herself on the armchair. The Count positioned himself behind her and removed his penis, which was already semi hard. Pulling her knickers to one side and bearing Melinda's vagina, the Count pushed his penis into her.

"Please be gentle." Melinda begged.

"The last thing I wish to do to you my sweet is hurt you. I am sorry it is so soon but over the last three months I have impregnated 500 women, who will soon bare my sons. Until my sons are of the age to reproduce I must work fast."

The Count kept his rhythm slow and sensitive, whilst explaining his behaviour.

"Well Roberto, you certainly know how to make a woman feel special."

Ignoring her comment he ejaculated his next son deep into her. As Melinda felt his sperm inject into her, a small tear formed and rolled down her cheek. She had just worked out that she was in fact a baby factory for the Count.

The Count removed himself from her and softly spoke,

"You will be helped with my sons, please don't hate me."

With this said he turned and vaporised into thin air.

Melinda sat still, taking the time to collate what had just happened. She was never known for her maths but she pondered about what was happening.

'So 500 baby boys every three months, who in only a short period can reproduce themselves, well you don't have to have a degree in maths to work out that in just a couple of years there will be many thousands of vampires.'

Leaning forward, Melinda reached to pick up the remote for the TV, turning it on as she sat back in her chair. Selecting the news channel she listened to the reporter,

"Police are concerned with a steady increase in unexplained killings nationwide. Links and investigation indicate a number of different serial killers, which seem to be geographically positioned. Police warn that this is the highest level of serial killer related incidents at any one time since records began."

Melinda still very much human couldn't help feel sad and angry for being part of what she understood was the Count's empire growing.

Chapter Nine

Tony quite exhausted from the night life activities began to understand why the myths about Vampires only surfacing at night had become confused with they cannot go out in daylight. Looking at his watch he noted it was 3pm and he was still in bed. He lay there for about thirty minutes and pondered,

'When this would all end. Was there any good that could come from this super race developing?'

The click of the kettle broke his deep and meaningful thoughts, as he found he had walked to the kitchen without even noticing the journey. Making his coffee really strong in an attempt to pick himself up he attended an itch on his left buttock.

"Tony, as always we have lots to do tonight, are you feeling strong and alert?"

"I wouldn't call it that but I'm up for it boss, don't worry. I've gotta ask Vamps, how long do we have to keep this pace up for?"

"Tony I have tried keeping the human population at a sensible number over the many of thousands of years, single handily. It has proved very inefficient; I have therefore made the decision that the time is right to unleash many sons to assist me with my conquest."

"So, as I asked before how long do you imagine all of this master plan of yours to take place?

"We have the advantage of being immortal Tony, humans life expectancy is only on average seventy years."

Getting a little frustrated that the counts answers were being more evasive than a politician. Tony grunted,

"I am not doing this for the next seventy years. I can tell you this for free pal."

The Count very disappointed with his answer cuffed Tony with a wide reverse right hook. From the force of the blow Tony flew several feet into the air landing the other side of the kitchen. Shaking his head to bring his vision back to single he thought,

'If I am immortal then what can he do?'

Rushing to his feet he charged the Count, screaming as he gained momentum, he felt like he could break down a wall. As he slammed into the granite kitchen centre unit, he realised the count had simply teleported to the other end of the unit.

"Tony this is not a fight you can win!"

Rubbing his head Tony noticed a speckle of blood on his palm. Jerking his head to a glass door cabinet to check his wound, he realised that he no longer had a reflection. Rubbing the wound again he found no more blood, as the open cut had already healed itself. Taking a deep breath Tony said,

"So this is it then, you don't answer any of my questions and if I step out of line you show me your might? If I am also immortal what is the point? We could do this all day."

"Tony, like a tiger when a cub gets too much it is brought back in line with a cuff. If the cub doesn't listen then it is simply food just like any other animal on the plain."

"So let me get this right if I want out, I got to get you to eat me!"

"It's that simple Tony, do you want out?"

Tony took a moment to consider his options,

"Nah, I'm good for now." Knowing he was beat he picked up his coffee and carried on as if the fight had not even taken place.

"Alright then, you won't answer my previous question but why do you only turn pretty woman?"

"Tony I did not choose not to answer your last question, there is a lot that can affect the outcome. I therefore cannot answer your question with any concrete certainty, time will tell. However your last question I can answer. One weakness I have noticed about man, over the many years, is that a man will almost do anything to reproduce with a pretty woman. This my friend, will be mans downfall."

"I see, so in a nutshell, your plan is for the women vamps to cull the race and for the men vamps to increase the population of Vampires."

"Correct Tony, this is the plan as you put it, in its entirety. Simple, but I believe it will be effective."

"Where is it tonight then?" Tony enquired.

"Liverpool, we need more penetration in this region."

Sitting in a busy bar in Liverpool, Tony's mind had gone into overdrive. He had so many questions but felt it was pointless asking them. Looking around the bar, it was heaving with attractive women. The plush relaxed feel to the bar attracted affluent, successful individuals who were all looking to keep their success and wealth within their middle upper class. It was also obvious that many of the women were out to find themselves a rich catch and were dressed to impress. Tony was not sure if he wanted to be part of this anymore,

'Shall I try and warn them of the Count, no they will think I have gone mad.'

"You look like you have the weight of the world on your shoulders, Tony?" the count asked interrupting his thoughts.

"Well, now I understand what you are up to, I have so many questions. I also have an idea which I think would make us some money at the same time as assist your conquest."

"Do tell Tony, do tell!"

"Well, one thing I have noticed as a plus to being turned from human to a Vampire is that you don't get ill. I was wondering what would happen if someone was seriously ill and you turned them, would they be cured of their illness?"

"No viruses can survive in my blood, so your theory would be correct. Why would I wish to help humans that are certain to die, how does this assist the conquest?"

"Well what I was thinking along with your 'Mans flaws' of sex always sells theory, is people also want to live forever. If someone was terminally ill and you put it to them that for a one off payment they could be cured, I am sure you would have people queuing up even if they knew the side effects."

"Wouldn't this put me very much in the spotlight?" the Count enquired,

"Yes I guess, I have not really thought the finer details through yet, I was just wondering."

"Money is man's other weakness, could we earn vast amounts of money from your idea Tony?"

"I guess, people would pay big figures to secure life."

"In return I would gain their soul. Tony, I like it, please think it through and let me know what we need to do next." Returning to the matter at hand the Count asked,

"What about that girl over there, the one with the T-shirt that says Just done it in Ibiza!"

The two returned to their nightly activities, Tony's conscience had taken a back seat as he now had his own master plan to concoct.

Remembering a ditto that Richard had once told him,

'Failing to plan, means you are planning to fail.' Tony had taken over the study of the manor with paperwork and brainstorming sheets scattered over his desk. He documented his idea into stages and covered areas such as marketing, Financials, start up costs, staff levels, which developed into a crude Business Plan. Perusing the detail of his scribbles he started to jot a 'To-do-list'

Agree Business Name
Set up sole trading bank account.
Design advert
Place advert in National papers
Order phone system
Recruit receptionist

Looking at his list he pondered, whilst he did, he attempted to roll his pen through his fingers in a magician like manner. Striking through his list he reorganised them into a different order, which he felt would be both

Phil J. Briggs

smarter and quicker to get the project off the ground. Pleased with his three hours effort, he ventured off to find the Count. Walking fast and with a bounce in his step, like a boy showing his father his first finished model plane, he investigated the Counts usual hiding spots. Drawing a blank he thought, 'Where can he be?' the only place he had not tried was the garden, Walking outside into the dull cloudy day, he saw the Count sitting by the BBQ.

"Vamps I've finished the plan, I reckon we can be up and running within a month. Here look."

The Count turned slowly and looked at Tony, his eyes had a sad glint to them.

"Thank you Tony, I will look over this and come back to you by the end of the day."

Tony felt that there was something wrong and asked,

"Are you ok? You don't look your usual I will rule the world kind of guy."

Smiling at Tony's question the Count paused and answered,

"Tony, you are the only friend I have ever had and yet yesterday I was willing to kill you. I am very jealous of man having companionship, I do get very lonely."

"Ah, you big softy. Come here and give Uncle Tone a cuddle."

Not understanding that Tony was in fact joking, the Count got up and opened his arms. Not daring to piss the Count off, Tony moved forward and embraced in a hug. Patting the Count on his back whilst saying,

"There, there, it's going to be alright." Tony couldn't help snigger a little and fought hard to hold back a huge grin.

Stepping apart, Tony looked the Count in the eye to check he was going to be ok and said,

"Right enough of that, back to work, got lots to be getting on with, let me know what you think of my plan ASAP?"

Turning, Tony walked briskly back to the manor, avoiding any further intermit moments with the Count.

Three long weeks had passed. Tony had been given full approval both methodically and financially to his plan. Tony's allocated budget of £30,000, which he initially thought to be overkill was already proving to be restrictive. He did not foresee just how much the national advertising campaign would cost to set up, nor for a telephone system that could handle the predicted amount of incoming calls.

Not deterred by this Tony placed his advert for a receptionist in the local paper. He had first suggested that this person should be a member of the Vampire clan and not a regular human. The Count did not agree with this suggestion and advised that the less this person knew about their kind the better. Also if this person truly believed that the cause to be for the good of the client, then this person would represent the Company in a more passionate and professional manner.

Tony had also suggested that he interview for this position alone, as he did not want the Count turning or feeding on the applicants. The Count again overruled his suggestion and insisted that he wanted to be present.

Two days had passed; the long awaited job vacancy was clearly advertised in the local rag. Tony hovered impatiently over the phone, willing for it to ring. After about an hour, Tony sat and reclined back into his cheap imitation leather executive chair. Pretending to be very important he fired up the solitaire program on his computer and angrily tapped away at his mouse.

"No wonder the country is in such a state, no one wants to bloody work anymore." He thought out loud. Just as the phone rang!

"Good afternoon, Life Savers, Tony speaking how may I help?"

Tony could not help but smile, as he felt quite 'executive' and the boss of his own little empire. Taking the details of the keen applicant, he arranged an interview slot for the following day.

As like busses, the phone rang a further five times, as fast as he could take the details, put another person on hold, another line started ringing.

"Phew! A bit of a mad moment there, all good though. Right, got six interviews for tomorrow." Tony had not realised that he was actually talking to himself when the Count entered the newly furnished office.

"I take it, things are going well Tony."

"Yes Boss, six likely candidates for tomorrow, first one is at 2pm so you are going to have be up early!"

The strange thing, the two were taking this business opportunity very seriously and more surprisingly they were actually a good partnership.

The Count had decided to wear a pair of blue Armani jeans, with a smart white polo shirt and a blue stripped jacket for the interviews. He looked like a true Director who had money but did not need to bow down to the usual shirt and tie brigade. Tony dressed in a light beige suit, white shirt and a paisley tie. This worked well as Tony did look like the understudy to the Count.

The first applicant turned up on time at 2pm, a lady in her late teens. She wore a tight dark blue skirt, which sat just above her knees, a white blouse, which was conveniently unbuttoned to show her cleavage. Although she had the opportunity to lose her chewing gum on the walk from the gate to the manor, she instead greeted Tony with,

"Hi I am Verona; I have come for an interview for the Receptionists position. Sorry could I trouble you for a bin? Forgot to lose my chewing gum!"

Tony had already made his mind up about Verona and answered,

"Please to meet you, yes here."

Again she did not strengthen her appearance by taking a bit of paper and placing the gum in it, instead she spat the gum into the bin.

"Please have a seat. I would like to introduce you to the Founder, Mr Roberto Drake."

Tony then entered into his questioning. This came quite natural to Tony and came across if he had been a Director for many years.

Verona answered all of Tony's questions correctly. She knew what he wanted to hear however the Count was not so easy to fool. About 15 minutes into the interview the Count interjected,

"So Verona, what is your highest score on Bubble Breaker?"

A bit baffled by this question Verona answered,

"Sorry I don't understand what relevance this has to this position."

"Were you not fired from your last job because all you did was play this game?"

Verona started to squirm,

"How do you know that?"

"I'll take that as a yes then, please shut the door as you leave." The Count ordered.

Very confused Verona got up; her face beetroot red she placed her C.V back into her folder.

"Well thank you for your time, I look forward to hearing from you." Verona said in desperation, as she shook their hands and retreated backwards out of the office.

As the door closed, Tony ripped into the Count,

"What are you doing?"

"I am sure we will get some strange inquisitive phone calls about our methods from our advert Tony. If she had handled the pressure to that question better and managed to swerve it or turned it into a positive, she would have got the job."

"I see, so it doesn't matter if she cannot work the phone system or anything that I have to ask only if she fits with you?"

"Tony don't be childish, trust me, I would hope you can do this by now."

The next four interviews went along the lines of Verona's, the Count blurting a question that only the person being interviewed could know. A bit down hearted with the calibre of candidates Tony had crossed everything for the last interview.

5.45pm and Lucy arrived on time.

Lucy had been through her introductions and sat patiently waiting for the interview to begin. She appeared smartly dressed in a nearly white trouser suit, which had been tailored to show off her fantastic figure. Although she was thirty-two Tony had put her age on appearance at twenty-six. He found her attractive but not drop dead gorgeous, although there was something about her that stimulated his interest.

Tony ranting off his usual questions, taking control of the interview, he noticed that Lucy had a very pleasant smile and found himself warming to her. About ten minutes passed when the count dropped his bombshell question.

"Lucy we only employ good looking women, do you have a problem with that?"

Not fazed by the Counts aggressive approach she composed herself and calmly spoke.

"I feel I am pleasant to the eye and therefore class myself as being within this category. The first impression to your clients is the receptionist, so I agree she requires to be of excellence."

Impressed with her answer the Count asked,

"When can you start Lucy?"

They spent the next thirty minutes agreeing salaries, start date and a brief overview of the activities of the business.

Lucy was of course interested to know how they intended to cure diseases that scientists have spent many years and vast sums on money trying to cure but agreed the less she knew the better.

As Lucy left, Tony looked at the Count with a look of parental care.

"Tony you don't have to worry I will leave her alone."

Pleased that the Count both understood Tony and that he again was offering his trust, Tony put out his hand to cement the deal. Moving his head a little to the left the Count was unsure what he should do.

"Here." Taking the Counts arm Tony placed the Counts hand in his.

"Now grip my hand firm, Aahh not too firm and not too sloppy and then we shake."

"This is human's way of promising to do something; it's called a Gentleman's Agreement."

"What have I promised to do?" asked the Count,

"Well we have just agreed that Lucy is our receptionist and you have agreed not to eat her."

"You humans are so complicated!" the count added.

Lucy turned up for her day's training, prior to the National Advert being released. As always she managed to dress classy but with a hint of mysterious sex appeal. Crossing her legs behind her desk, her nude coloured hold ups rubbed slightly, making a quiet static sound. Tony locked his attention to this graceful procedure, almost as if he were a laser tracker for a missile.

"Lucy please do make yourself comfortable and familiarise with your surroundings. I will come back in half an hour. I have some important business to attend to, after which I will be all yours."

"Thank you, Mr? Sorry I don't know your surname?"

"Don't worry, please call me Tony. Oh before I forget, is it ok to pay you your month's salary in advance. As a new venture the last thing I want is for you to worry about if you are going to get paid."

"I really don't think that will be a problem!" Lucy answered.

"Cool, I will organise the cash on my return." With this Tony walked off towards the entertainment room. He had suddenly developed a 'Blackman's Ghetto' type of walk, crammed full of confidence, as he had decided he really liked Lucy.

About an hour later, Tony woke from his snooze and quickly realised that he had overslept.

"Shit!" he said as he acknowledged his hair was a mess and he was in desperate need of cleaning his teeth. Rushing to his en-suite, he performed a guy strip wash, which involves removing as little clothing as possible but cleaning all of your personal areas.

Sliding into the reception area, Tony grabbed the door frame, in an attempt to stop himself shooting on past Lucy's desk and straight out the manor door.

"Hi, really sorry got caught up in a conference call. You know a Salesman never sleeps."

"Really it's no problem Tony; it has given me the time I need to get to know where everything is."

"Cool, I think the best thing to start with is if I show you the advert being released tomorrow in all the National papers. You will know what people are calling about and also know what its content is etc."

Placing the approved proof in front of her, it read,

Do you have a terminal illness?
Would you like to be cured?

Techniques, 100% successful Guaranteed.
Only 'One Off' payment (£10,000)
Payment plans available.
50% Deposit required to secure treatment, remainder due on satisfaction of treatment.
1St five clients treated free.
If you are interested in the above please call
TEL: 0870 169 ####
Between 2pm & 8pm

The small print read, the above treatments and procedures have not been approved by any medical board. In the interest of making this service available now, this service is only available on a private basis. Side effects will be experienced.

Lucy looked up from reading the advert and asked, "Is this a scam?"

"No it is real. It is a painful process so you will hear screams coming from the back room, this is normal don't worry."

"Wow you guys will be millionaires for sure."

"We of course look after our staff who got the business off the ground. Is there anything else you wish to know?" Tony asked,

"No I think that is about it."

"Well let's get some lunch then. My shout!"

"Ok." Lucy replied in a sheepish voice, looking at her watch, which read 4pm.

Lucy arrived the following day very much pumped up and vibrant. Positioning her chair she felt that today was going to be a busy one. She had thought of nothing else the night before and really wanted to be a part of this exciting service. Checking her notes from the previous days training, she felt confident that she could do well. Looking at her watch, she noted it was 1.45pm. She thought,

'I'd better go and spend a penny as I think the phones will be off the hook come 2pm'.

As she pulled her knickers down and lowered to sit, she heard phone line one leap into life.

"Damn, let me have a tinkle first."

Returning to her desk she looked at the extension board of the phone system, all twenty lights were furiously flashing. Lucy suddenly remembered that,

'Tony never did give her that advance.'

"Good Afternoon, Life Savers. How can I help?"

A frail voice spoke on the other end,

"Is this true can you cure me of Cancer?"

"Yes Madam, when can you come in and see our consultant?"

As fast as Lucy could answer a call, book the caller the next available time slot, the extension board would again fill up.

Lucy realised that it was nearly 7pm and she had not eaten, nor stopped. She also had not seen hide or hair of the two Directors, when Tony appeared.

"Hi Lucy, how's it going?"

"The phones have not stopped all day; you are booked solid for the next three weeks."

"Excellent news! Sorry, I forgot to give you your pay yesterday." Tony said as he handed over a brown envelope stuffed with cash.

"I know you have not stopped all day, why don't you call it a day Lucy. Put the system into night service." The Count instructed as he entered the room.

"Thanks, it is appreciated." Lucy replied, frantically pushing the buttons to put the phone system into night service and shutting down her PC.

"See you tomorrow!" Tony added.

"Night." Lucy said as she bolted for the door,

"Well a good response I believe?" the Count exclaimed.

"Yes Boss, you won't be going hungry for a bit."

"Tony I am very pleased with your idea; I would have never of thought of it in a million years."

"Well I am the brains of this operation. You may be the good looking one but as I have always said, Upstairs for thinking, downstairs for dancing!"

Locking up the office there was a great feel of success and happiness, this was a new sensation to the Count and he liked it. As they wandered back into the domestic section of the Manor, Tony asked,

"Are you out and about tonight?"

Yes of course Tony, I have to feed. What time is our first patient tomorrow?"

"Early doors, I think, 2pm."

Chapter Ten

1.30pm the following day and Mrs Bailey arrived at the Manor as instructed. She had a driver allocated as she had been instructed she would not be able to drive home.

As she walked into the reception, Lucy stood to greet her. Lucy's face struggled to hold a warm inviting expression as she was surprised that Mrs Bailey was only in her mid thirties. When she had spoken to her previously Lucy had put her down as being at least fifty plus.

"Hello Mrs Bailey, good to see you, please do take a seat. The partners will be with you shortly."

Mrs Bailey sat patient, nervous of what the treatment might entail.

Tony entered the waiting room, fully charged and full of beans.

"Good Afternoon Mrs Bailey", he spoke slightly louder than he normally would, his tone very confident.

Mrs Bailey struggled to her feet, her friend assisted by supporting her weight under one arm. She had not long had chemo therapy, which was still knocking her sideward.

"Please walk this way." Tony said as he gestured his arm towards the back office.

Helping Mrs Bailey to her seat which was positioned in front of the Counts desk, Tony then closed the door behind her.

The Count looked at Mrs Bailey with a penetrating stare and said,

"I can guarantee you will walk out of here healed of your ailment but I need to explain the side effects to this treatment."

"Well there's no such thing as a free lunch is there?" Mrs Bailey nervously answered.

The Count looked at Tony as they both smirked, as they knew differently.

"Mrs Bailey, the side effects you will experience will change your life forever. You will however be able to live a normal life but you will feed differently. Do you accept this in return for curing you of Cancer?"

"Yes, I can eat through a straw if I need to." Mrs Bailey replied.

The Count stood and moved in a circular action to position himself behind Mrs Bailey. In a deep soft voice the Count confirmed,

"You could liken it to a straw. You will shortly feel a sharp sting in your neck, don't worry this is the treatment working."

Locating his whereabouts by his voice she turned to look, as she did the Count lunged in and struck the other side of her neck. As the Counts fangs sank deep into her jugular Mrs Bailey let out a loud scream. Drinking hard the Count let out a muffled growl, which sounded over the top of her scream.

Startled by Mrs Baileys scream, Lucy dropped the handset and fumbled to pick it up. "Sorry about that Mr Steward, I dropped the telephone, do continue."

Whilst keeping a calm and collective telephone manner, Lucy looked at Mrs Bailey's friend and gave an expression of concern.

Only drinking enough blood, the Count injected his own into her to turn her. Removing his bite from her neck, he licked his lips and joked,

"I'm gonner like this job, I can tell."

Mrs Bailey briefly drifted in and out of consciousness, her head became too heavy for her to support.

"You need to rest Mrs Bailey, you are cured. The next couple of days will be strange but I will be in contact to help you. Thank you for your business, Tony will take it from here."

Tony leapt to his feet and offered Mrs Bailey his hand.

"Come on, this way."

Walking back into the waiting room, a very worried friend stood,

"Is she ok?" he asked.

"Yes the procedure went perfectly, she will need to rest for the next couple of days, then she will be as good as new. Oh, once she has recovered we may ask to use her contact details for nervous customers. I am sure she will give us a glowing reference. Drive safely."

Tony shut the door behind them and looked at Lucy and said in a jovial voice,

"Another satisfied customer. Who do we have next?"

Lucy indicated that she was just finishing her call and would be free to introduce the next client.

Using this method the Count was able to feed eight times a day and earn £80,000, in the process. The Count had adopted a very stiff policy regarding non-payment and always made it very clear to his clients that he could easily take the life back if the 2nd payment was not met. With turning over just shy of half a million a week, Tony's idea also enabled the Count to replenish his wealth. With turning the population output increased to eight a day, his culling team was also increasing at a vast rate.

Mrs Bailey rested as instructed, drifting in and out of a coma like sleep for at least a day after her treatment. Her friend who had accompanied her to Life Savers, agreed to stay with her for a couple of days. Gerald, her friend looked at her whilst she slept, he thought,
'She did look slightly healthier already'.
He sat in a fold up camping chair, which he had the foresight to bring. Looking around her bedroom he became quite bored as the non-personal magnolia painted walls gave him no inspiration of thought. Looking at a photo of Mrs Bailey and her ex husband, which she kept on display, he thought,
'What a rat her husband was. Leaving her and proceeding with a divorce as her illness worsened.'
Gerald never did like her husband and always thought that he would have been a better husband to her. His thoughts were disturbed; Mrs Bailey was ranting and thrashing in her deep sleep. Like all the others the Count was talking to her telepathically and informing her of what she had become.

Stirring from her deep sleep, Mrs Bailey licked her lips and made a slight moaning sound. Slowly opening her eyes she flinched from the bright daylight beaming in.

"Take your time; I'll get you some water." Gerald said.

Arriving back fully armed with a plastic beaker of water, he handed it to Mrs Bailey. She had now woken and was sitting up with pillows stuffed behind her back.

"Well if you don't mind me saying so, you do look a lot better; I think the treatment has worked."

In a gravelly voice Mrs Bailey replied,

"Thank you Gerald, you are a good friend, you have always been there for me. I think I did marry the wrong man. Come I need a cuddle."

Gerald lent over the bed and embraced her with an affectionate cuddle. He was happy with the last statement and still believed there might be a chance for him and her getting together.

"Sorry" Mrs Bailey softly spoke,

"What are you sorry about?" Gerald enquired.

As Gerald waited for his answer, Mrs Bailey sank her fangs into his neck. Gerald's eyes wide with both shock and pain he thought,

'Why, what have I ever done wrong?'

Mrs Bailey snarled slightly as she drank him dry. Releasing her bite, Gerald slowly rolled off the bed into a curled up heap on the floor.

Mrs Bailey's eyes burned bright, her feed had finished her treatment. She felt the life of Gerald rush round her veins, taking a deep breath she felt fantastic. Looking at Gerald's lifeless body, she looked up at the photo of her ex husband. She knew whom her next feed would be on.

With their first week of trading over, Tony looked at the Count and said.

"Well partner, a good job done. I would suggest we celebrate but you must be a pig in poo at the moment."

The Count leant back into the sofa, pressing the TV control to on.

"Tony, I think your idea is a fantastic one, but this is only the start."

Looking at the TV, Tony didn't really want to dwell too much on what had just been said. Extending the recliner of the chair he crossed his legs and started to get comfortable. Drifting off into his own little world Tony asked,

"Do you get fat if you overfeed?"

The Count laughed whilst shaking his head,

"Tony you do make me laugh, I sometimes wonder what goes on in that head of yours. No I do not get fat, I can just go longer without having to feed."

"So what happens if you are unable to feed?"

"I am able to hibernate for many years without feeding. My family however cannot and would naturally die of starvation, within a couple a weeks."

"So if you were in hibernation and you weren't disturbed, how long would it take for you to starve?"

As Tony was naturally a curious kind of guy, the Count did not think there was anything malicious in this form of questioning and answered.

"Approximately 150 years, if I was fully fed before hibernation."

"Ooh is that all?" Tony joked. His eyes had started to become heavy and he felt himself fighting to not drift off. As he did, he took great comfort in knowing that at least the Count could die, he didn't know how yet but he knew he could.

Six months had passed and Melinda was nearly ready to give birth to her third baby boy. Leon looked like a healthy four year old although he was only six months old. Michael her second son, was also feeding well and growing rapidly. Melinda's perfectly formed breasts now looked like they had gone several rounds with Mohamed Ali. She had therefore decided to adopt a new feeding method for her sons that night.

Using her usual techniques to attract clientele, she sat patiently at the bar. Taking longer than usual she looked at her watch absorbing that it was 9.15pm. A little concerned she looked around the vibrant busy venue. As she did she felt a twitch in her stomach and thought,

'No not now, got to feed first.'

A slight feeling of panic trembled over her body as she realised the pressure that was upon her. Although she did not need to be picky as she was not looking for breeding material but instead a simple meal, she found that if the man came to her it was a sure thing. She had to remain patient, although her senses were going haywire. As she fought simply leaping on the next person that passed, her waiting was over.

A man in his late thirties nervously spoke,

"When is it due?"

"Oh not long now it could be any time soon. The only trouble is being pregnant makes me really horny!"

"Wow I was going to ask if you had a boyfriend etc, but I think it is quite clear you need a good rogering."

"You are a wise man, you know what, most guys would try a bit of smooth chat with several drinks to get the same result."

Interrupting, the man said,

"Your place or mine?"

"Mine, but I must warn you I really need satisfying, not just a quickie. Are you alright to stay the night or do you have to shoot off back to the wife?"

"No she thinks I am staying overnight on business so I am all yours. Let's get out of here. Is your place far?"

"Not really it's just around the corner."

Putting her arm around him she led him in the direction of her apartment. Turning the key to her front door, she peeked through the opening door, to ensure her kids were temporarily out of sight.

"Come in, make yourself comfortable."

Sitting in an armchair he watched Melinda with great interest. Even though she was heavily pregnant she was still looking sexy.

Moving slowly towards the man, she looked at him with seductive eyes, which stirred his groin area, taking his penis from soft to a lazy lob. Striding his open legs she confidently lowered her crotch to touch his trousers. Slowly grinding down on his member she gently kissed his neck. Locking in a deep passionate kiss, the man firmly thrust his manhood up into her moist knickers. As he gazed into her beautiful blue eyes his warm feeling of lust suddenly turned to terror. Letting out a loud cry he looked down at his hands, focussing on his wrists he could not believe to see two boys locked onto his main arteries and sucking his blood. His initial reaction to shake the kids off was disturbed, as he looked at Melinda.

Her face once perfect in all aspects now looked like a wolf defending its young. Her long fangs fully bared, with her mouth wide open she growled in a cat like manner. Her eyes glowing a piercing white the man knew he was in trouble.

"Get off me you fucking freak!"

Looking at her boys to understand if they were full, she lunged at the man's neck. Taking a large bite, she sank her fangs deep into his neck. Jigging her bite slightly, the man close to passing out with pain uttered,

"What about my wife and kids?"

Ignoring his question Melinda forced his arms beside his shoulders pinning him in place. A sound of her sucking his blood from his body filled the room, as Melinda finished him off. The boys new to this, took little nips at his calve muscles, almost as if they were playing with their kill. Releasing her bite and licking her lips she said in a firm commanding voice.

"Leave him, I have told you not to play with your food. Go to bed I will be in to tuck you in shortly."

Melinda took her time to dismount from the man and thought,

'What do I do with his body?' Feeling content and full she subconsciously caressed her breasts, as she was pleased the boys were no longer feeding from her. Focusing back on what she was going to do with the sapped body. A knock on her door broke her train of thought. Bolting her head towards the direction of the door, she quickly turned her head back to the body.

"Shit, bet it's the fuzz." she ranted.

Before she could think what she should do, a stronger knock focused her attention back on opening the door.

Placing the safety chain in its locking plate she slowly opened the door, just enough to use one eye to greet the caller. Melinda asked,

"What seems to be the problem? It is 10.30pm you know."

"I know what time it is Melinda, my name is Tony. Roberto sent me over to help you with an unwanted visitor."

Understanding it was safe, Melinda unhitched the safety chain and opened the door.

As Tony came into full view, Tony looked at Melinda and thought to himself,

'Nice going Count, she is well fit.'

Shutting the door behind him, Tony looked around the room to find the body. As he watched Melinda take the man's hands and drag him from out of the chair, he noticed that she had a dim yellow glow silhouetting her body. Blinking his eyes several times to clear his view he looked back at Melinda. What he saw was no different the glow was definite and not part of his imagination.

"Here let me." Tony said as he advanced towards Melinda.

Picking the man up in a fireman's lift Tony asked if she had any black bin liners. Melinda returned from the kitchen armed with two large heavy duty green garden waste sacks.

"Will these do?" she asked not sure if black was important or not.

"Perfect, put one over his feet."

Covering his body with the two sacks, Tony turned to Melinda and said in a cheeky voice,

"I suppose a blowjob is out of the question?"

Shaking her head with a smile on her face she replied,

"Tony just get rid of the body!"

"Hey just checking, I need some form of payment for helping you out!"

"Maybe another night, I am tired and would like an early night. I got the feeling this thing will be popping out of me at any moment soon."

No problem, don't get used to this, I am only helping out until you have dropped. Then you're back on your own, I will of course give you the heads up on disposing of the bodies."

"Thanks Tony, are you sure you want me near your bits and bobs, I might get peckish."

"I am immortal, you can try if you like. I don't fancy your chances if you did though!"

Tony turned and negotiated the door with the man slumped across his shoulder.

"Catch ya later!" He said as he disappeared down the stairs.

Tony had managed to park near to Melinda's flat and had already removed the seats making it easy to simply throw the body in the back. Casually, he walked with the body slung over his shoulder, he thought the more natural he was the less chance someone would look at him with any suspicion.

Another idea that Tony had, was with some of the profits from Life Savers, they had decided to invest into renting the facility of using the incinerators from the local Pet Cemetery. They had managed to convince the owners of strategically positioned cemeteries, that they were performing medical tests with diseased animals and required to hygienically dispose of the remains.

Arriving at the Cemetery, although for pets it still felt creepy. Tony who still thought of himself as very much human looked around nervously. He tended to forget that he really did not need to worry at all as there was only one thing that could harm him. Opening the boot he pulled on the feet of the man, bringing him nearly all the way out from the car he placed the feet on the floor. Placing his shoulder in the man's midriff Tony jerked the man back into a fireman's lift position. As he walked to the entrance he found he was humming the melody to 'Somebody's Watching Me' by Michael Jackson. It was probably because the dance cover versions video, was set in a cemetery with zombie's break dancing in routine.

Entering the pin code for the alarm he opened the entrance door, he had managed to get the keys out of his pocket without having to remove the body from his shoulder. Walking to the incinerator, he turned and tried to moon walk backwards, still humming the melody he performed a human mix and turned the tune into Thriller, another well known Michael Jackson hit.

"Oww!" he sung, as he used his free hand to grab his crotch. Crossing his feet he spun round pretending he was actually Michael himself. As he spun round the centrifugal force flung the man's foot out, knocking over a desktop holder full of pens.

"Shit, I'll pick them up later." He muttered, thinking it would be easier without the stiff on his shoulder.

Tony placed the body on the conveyor belt of the incinerator and paused to try and remember how to operate it. The owner did go into great lengthy detail but Tony as usual, his mind was elsewhere. He remembered that the big red button was to stop it but couldn't see the obvious green button to start it. Nodding his head from left to right, still to 'Thriller' he looked at the controls. The small panel had only a handful of buttons but he did remember that they had to be run in sequence to activate the bone mashers and chopping knifes in the correct order. Taking his time to ensure he recalled the instructions of the owner, he pressed three buttons in random order as he could not remember what to do. He did remember that the temperature of the incinerator had to be set to maximum.

"Sorry me old china, hopefully you will be dust at the end and not a beaten up mess."

Tony watched the body slowly drift off into the entrance of the monstrosity of a machine and turned to pick up the pens.

Melinda was correct with her prediction, as her water broke she knew she needed to attend hospital. She was mindful the midwife maybe the same one and did not want to cause suspicion popping out babies every three months. She had managed to get a different one last time, so she thought the probability was not in her favour. She also was worried about leaving the kids, as she would not be able to leave them with a friend and say,

"If they get hungry pop out and get them the first person you meet!"

Just then a knock at the door broke her thoughts, opening it without any additional security, Tony came into view. He was terminating his call from his mobile but looked up to Melinda to acknowledge her.

"Yes Roberto, I am here now, I will look after the kids whilst she pops another one out. I guess you will be here in a bit. Yeah ok, cheers."

"Hi, I knew you would not be able to go the night without seeing me again." Tony boldly said.

"Go on off you go, I will look after your tribe. When were they last fed?"

Melinda catching her breath from a deep contraction said,

"Not long ago, you just took the body away!"

"Oki doki, then." Tony replied, giving Melinda the impression that he was capable and in control.

Melinda was gone no more than six hours when she returned with another beautiful baby boy.

Unlocking the door she entered her flat, looking frantically to see if the Count was waiting.

"All go ok?" Tony asked, whilst flicking the next channel of the TV.

"Yes thanks, is Roberto here?" she asked timidly.

"Not yet, he is a busy chap you know. His diary is fully rammed for the next one hundred years."

Tony's attention had turned to the news, as the presenter explained that stabbings and serial murders were now a daily affair. Bodies were being found all over the place, the Police have no explanations for the dramatic increase of fatalities.

Tony laughed quietly and muttered,

"It is going to get a lot worse, a lot worse, before it can get better."

Melinda looked at Tony with a puzzled face and asked,

"How can it get better? Do you know something I don't?"

Before Tony could answer, the Count materialised, "Melinda my sweet, let me look at my new son."

Moving the blanket that was surrounding his face she pointed her new son at the Count.

"Ah you are going to be a handsome little tiger, aren't you Jason."

Melinda never did get the chance to tell the Count what name she had given his sons. He always used his telepathic powers to search her mind first.

"Tony would you be so kind to take baby Jason and mind him for a little bit. Melinda please join me in the bedroom."

Melinda unwillingly handed Jason to Tony. Her face similar to a child who really doesn't like their medicine, she shuffled her feet in the direction of the bedroom.

Chapter Eleven

Two years later, the year 2008 and Life Savers now have over 3,000 satisfied customers of which, were all feeding and breeding as of their gender. With the hard work the Count had put in before the company's formation and his sons popping out all over the Country. The Vampire race was becoming a serious might with its numbers growing in excess of twelve thousand.

Rumours and speculation about Life Savers methods and success ratio for curing diseases that scientists had spent many years trying to cure was attracting attention from the press and media. All patients understood that they were not to disclose any of the treatment process. Besides talking about it would only attract attention to themselves. It was made very clear that it was not a good idea to discuss the process to anyone. The only proof that Life Savers methods were actually working was the medical files of Life Savers clients, who had all been diagnosed as terminal. The fact that all of Life Savers patients no longer wished to have any further assistance or medication and were all still living was of course causing a hoo-ha. For this to be detected on the sonar of the NHS meant that there had to be something in Life Savers methods.

This was one of the Counts initial concerns but felt that the return delivered from this public method outweighed the risks from investigation.

The paparazzi camped outside the gates to the manor most mornings hoping to get a shot of the Proprietors coming or going. It was only a matter of time that they would uncover that the previous owner of the manor had died without a will. His assets were frozen by the authorities and lost in the abyss of files, waiting for the next beneficiary to be found.

"What are we going to do about the press?" Tony asked, as they were in between clients.

"Tony, normally the press is a good thing but in our situation, we really do not need the attention they are bringing."

"Yeah, so what are we gonna do?"

"The press are a separate species; animals like us feeding off their next victim. They do not care who they crush, as long as they get their story. I have of course experienced their interest over the many years but they have evolved so much. With your new digital world their efforts are maximised and at such speed."

"If I didn't know you better I would say you are scared of them Vamps!" Tony took a step backwards and cringed slightly as he said this.

"If you fear nothing Tony, you become vulnerable. Who is our next client?"

"Mrs Brockenhurst, she is the last for the day. Look we have been at this for nearly three years solid now. Shall we go out tonight and just enjoy ourselves, no conquest no feeding. Just two lads having a laugh, a few beers, well me anyway and of course shag the arse off a couple of babes."

Rising from his chair with a stern posture, the Count advanced towards Tony. Keeping eye contact the Count moved directly in front of Tony. Looking down at Tony the Counts face evil with hate he broke into a smile and said.

"You should see your face. You look like you are going to give birth to a Tortoise head. I think this is an excellent idea, let's let our hair down."

"Cool, I need a night off."

It was a strange notion of Tony's, as the night would not really be any different for him. If he had said 'shall we stay in and order Pizza and watch a DVD,' this would be a break from the norm. The Count found this strange and found himself for the first time doubting Tony's intentions.

Although his intentions were totally innocent, he was excited about going out with no agenda. Putting on his lucky black & white stripe pants he thought,

'What do I need luck for? If I want a woman all I have to do is let the Count go and chat her up.'

All the same, he still wanted to look his best and picked out his favourite Italian shirt and white fitted jeans.

Almost jumping the last three steps of the staircase, Tony glided across the lobby and shimmied into the

Kitchen. Clicking his fingers and walking as if he were in a rap video, he said,

"You ready to Part-tay."

The Count looked methodical for a second and looked up with a boyish charm and said,

"You betcha!"

The Count was immaculately clothed in a designer ensemble, which indicated wealth whilst providing a glimpse view of his chiselled physique.

Due to the success of the Life Savers, Tony had secured an Aston Martin DB8 for his company car. He had been advised of the obvious tax advantages of the company leasing such a car and felt it rude to argue with the facts.

Revving the powerful engine, it rattled slightly as it was still cold. After just a few minutes, the purr to the engine tone made Tony smile. Dumping the clutch he put the pedal to the metal and sped down the shingle road, snaking towards the private road and main gates. Pressing the remote for the gates Tony said,

"Them Paps better not be in my way, as I am not stopping for no one."

Hearing the perfectly tuned roar from the Aston, the Paparazzi got into position. By the time the gates were fully open, Tony was nearly upon them. Blipping the engine revs as he changed down into 2nd gear, he checked the path was clear and floored it. Leaving the Manor at a speed of approximately 50mph, the Paps tried their best to get the shot. White multiple flashes illuminated the dark of the evening that was drawing in, as twenty Paparazzi took as many photo's as they possibly could, as the Aston sped past.

"Eat my dust!" Tony chuckled, engaging third gear.

Dave one of the Paps looked anxiously at the LCD screen of his Nikon camera. Flicking through the eighteen shots he had managed to take, his face turned from one of excitement to a puzzled expression. He had managed to take five clear shots of the interior of the Aston, which should have revealed the identity of the owners. What he saw appeared that the car was remote controlled. He could clearly see the light brown leather seats of both the driver and passengers; no one was in the car. Not alone, several of the other Paps looked at their cameras in disbelief.

Tony took care to park the car, which was situated five minutes from Southampton town centre. A passer by stopped to watch, as Tony slowly nudged forward and backwards to fit in the space.

"You're driving back, I am getting plastered." Tony stated.

The Count did not argue but didn't feel it the right time to tell Tony, that he had never driven before.

Like a boy with a new toy, Tony marched towards the first bar in sight. As he did he noticed a person walking on the other side of the road, who had a dim yellow glow. Tony had decided that vampires could spot other vampires and asked the Count,

"It's handy having the glow thing going on, so you can tell the vamps from the humans."

Confused the Count asked,

"What are talking about Tony?"

"Don't you see it; look at the chap across the road look how he glows."

The Count looked long and hard,

"Tony I do not see any glow as you put it. I am intrigued as to why you can and I do not! "

"You can see if it is one of your sons right?"

"No Tony, to me all is food, so I do not need to know. I can smell if they have my blood though. I have to be close but visually no I cannot tell"

"I knew there had to be some way otherwise you may undo all of your hard work!"

As they marched towards the bar the Count stepped back a little and pondered about what Tony had just said. For reasons unknown to Tony, this worried the Count immensely. Standing at the bar Tony looked around the venue. It was not a swanky polished hip place but it had a good feel to it. The music was at a good volume and a rendition of old school Dance mix was playing.

In a vibrant upbeat mood Tony jigged to the beat as he waited to be served.

"Can you feel the music?" Tony asked placing his arms in front of his body and bouncing them to the rhythm.

"Tony you do make me laugh, music does nothing for me."

"Oh come on you old fart, I've got you to dress funky, I've got you holding down a steady job, I am sure I can get you to slide like a cool mother fucker."

Smiling the Count thought about Tony's achievements and replied,

"If you can make me enjoy this noise, you can pat yourself on the back."

"I'll do my best, maybe not tonight but I will get you strutting your stuff if it kills me." Tony remarked.

Ordering a pint of lager, Tony supped it back as if it was the last drink on earth. He was certainly on a mission to lose a few brain cells and wanted to really let his hair down.

Turning round to face the venue he jigged and found it quite funny to sing loudly the chorus to the song that was playing,

"I've got the power!" (Sung by Snap)

Thrusting his hips to the left and then to the right, he copied the movements from the video. Feeling as if he could take on the world he confidently looked around the bar for hot women. To his surprise he saw two women, which fitted the bill. Both of them had a dim yellow glow surrounding them. He thought,

'Wow first bar and already two vamps on the prowl.'

Keeping his eye on them he did not realise that this was giving one of them the wrong impression. Boldly one of the women, who was about 5' 6" slim, blonde hair and well endowed walked up to Tony. As she got closer, she started to join in with the rhythm and sexily moved in time with Tony. Placing her hands on his chest she leant into him and said,

"Hey handsome, haven't seen you in here before?"

Gently taking her hands he moved them from his chest and placed them at her side, looking her straight in the eye he said,

"As much as I would love to do you, you look very hot. You are wasting your time with me. I am not your next meal, try someone else!"

Taking a big step back the woman looked startled and felt vulnerable.

"What?" she gasped,

"Go on get out of here." Tony barked and turned away from her to look for any other potential babes. The woman scared of being exposed did as Tony asked and left the bar.

Several bars later, Tony was quite merry and had consumed six pints. He turned to the count and asked,
"Why don't you have a drink with me, it would be cool to see you pissed."
"Tony, you know I cannot stomach lager, anyway I'm driving remember?!!"
As the count answered Tony, he looked down at his right foot, which for reasons unknown to him had started tapping to the beat of the music.
"Damn you Tony."
"What did I do?"
"Look what you have done, you've made my foot start doing things it has never done before."
"Alrighty then" Tony said, as his jigging became a dance floor move. This involved his feet moving and sliding fast, which made him look like he was moving without taking any steps.
"It's only a matter of time old boy and you will be body popping your thousand year old ass off." Tony laughed.

Although Tony was enjoying the evening, he felt it was not complete, as he had not spotted any women really worth chatting up. He decided to try one further bar to try and find his Cinderella, if unsuccessful he would call it a night.
"Come let's try one more bar, if there are no hot lovely's, I'm gonna call it a night!"

"What do you seek, Tony?" the Count asked.

"Well a fine looking babe, who can suck start a leaf blower."

"No seriously what are you pursuing?"

"Look I am thirty one now, I am looking for a beautiful lady who I can spend time with and have a balanced conversation with. Someone I can make love to not just meaningless sex."

At this point it made sense to the Count why Tony wanted to go out socially and not professionally, which reassured him.

"So you are looking for a lady companion, to grow old with?"

"Well I guess that is along the right lines, she has to be fit though."

"Tony, I once like you felt this way but let me tell you, when you have seen many loved ones come and go you will learn not to share your heart. This is the one downside to being immortal."

Walking to the next bar, Tony expressed,

"Well that has put a downer on my evening, thanks we might as well go back to the manor and order in pizza and rent a DVD."

As Tony said this he noticed a man walking towards them who had the glow surrounding him.

"Look out, it's one of your clan!"

Before the Count could answer, the man was upon Tony, as he passed his shoulder engaged with Tony's. Tony and the Count kept on walking, without taking any notice to the man's territorial behaviour.

"Oi, you got a problem?" the man aggressively asked.

Tony first turned and widened his stance. Clenching one fist he replied,

"You may think you are a superhero but trust me you do not have what it takes. Walk on and go feed on someone else."

The man a little surprised with Tony reaction was not intimidated and marched towards Tony.

The Count looked at Tony with a puzzled face and asked,

"What are you doing Tony?"

"If a man challenges you in the street it is fighting talk."

"Oh, allow me." the count added,

The Count stepped in front of Tony, he looked hard and direct at the oncoming man. Squinting his eyes they glowed white. This was a type of warning shot to the man, obviously the Count did not want to harm a fellow vampire but like Tony thought he needed putting in his place.

"Do as he says." The Count instructed the man.

"Fuck off, old man or I will hurt you as well!"

Stopping a foot from the Count the man changed into his vampire form and hissed violently. Bringing his arms up in bird like fashion he lunged his face forward fangs extended. Laughing at the man the Count looked at Tony and said,

"Do you want to take him or shall I?"

"No he is all yours boss, mess him up!"

With that the Count slammed an open hand into the man's chest. Sending the man flying backwards at an immense speed, the Count thought this would be enough to indicate to the man that he was out gunned.

Any normal man receiving a blow such as this would certainly be dying of internal organ failure. The man lay in a heap about 5inches from the wall that had stopped his travel. He lay motionless for about a minute as his vampire DNA healed his damaged organs. Waking from his injury his eyes opened wide. Rising from his cowering position he looked at the Count with a new anger.

"I am immortal you can not harm me, I will now kill you slowly, you should have ran whilst you had the chance." the man stated.

Finding this man's actions quite amusing the Count extended his arm and offered out his hand. With his first and second finger he made an enticing gesture and said,

"Bring it on numb nuts."

Like a red rag to a bull, the man ran towards the Count. As he entered striking distance he leapt with vigour, hoping to bowl the Count over.

Taking a long step backwards, the Count lowered himself into a martial art like stance. As he did this he removed an 18inch serrated bladed knife from the lower back region of his trousers. As the knife came free from its metal sheath, it made a clear and cutting metallic sound, which could not be mistaken for any other object.

The man zooming in towards the Count, face dropped as he saw the glisten of the shiny blade. Taking a clean swiping motion the Count decapitated the man with one swift action. As the Count span and regained his stance, the man's head bounced and settled near Tony's feet. Almost in slow motion, Tony watched the body slowly land a couple of feet from the head.

Tony a little disturbed by this, gave the head a gentle kick to roll it further away from him and the body. Taking a big gulp Tony asked,

"Will it grow back?"

"No Tony, this is the only sure way to kill a vampire."

"What, even me?" Tony inquisitively asked.

"Yes Tony, you and also myself. If we lose our heads we are no longer immortal."

Removing a handkerchief from his trouser pocket, the Count wiped the blood from his blade.

"Such a waste!" he muttered, as he homed the blade back into the sheath.

"Let's get out of here, the last thing we need is the fuzz catching us." Tony ranted.

A feeling of uncertainty rushed over Tony, as he suddenly felt quite vulnerable. Now knowing he could in fact be quite easily slaughtered, he walked in an urgent way losing his previous confidence, back towards the car.

Starting the engine of the Aston, the Count looked repeatedly over the controls and wished he had paid more attention to Tony when he was driving.

"Ok, how do you pilot this thing?" He asked.

"Don't tell me you've never driven before?"

"Never had to Tony, I just normally teleport to where I want to go. This looks fun though so let's have a go!"

Shaking his head, before holding it in both hands, Tony said,

"We're screwed!"

Taking a deep breath and trying to remain calm he explained,

"Place you left foot on the far left pedal. That's it, now press the pedal down. Using your left hand put the car into first gear. Ok that's good. Now using your mirrors check there are no cars coming, put your indicator on and slowly increase the revs with your right foot."

What? sorry you going to have to be a little clearer than that."

"For fucks sake, get out of the car and I will drive!"

Releasing the depressed clutch pedal, the Count opened the door to exit the car. Stalling the Aston, the car leapt forward, catching the count's shoulder blade. Taking no notice of the car striking him, he closed his eyes as he made contact to a newly turned lady, telepathically. This was a task he normally performed without the need to focus his thoughts. As the car struck him this momentarily distracted him from his ongoing communications.

Although very much over the limit, Tony felt he could drive the car back to the manor without causing an accident. The problem was a car so highly tuned as the Aston, it was hard keeping it to any of the lower speed limits. Trying his best to concentrate on the speedometer and keeping the car from veering erratically, Tony was unable to talk and drive.

The Count thought it might be fun to purposely antagonise Tony and started bombarding him with questions as he drove.

"So the clutch pedal makes the car go forward then?"

"Or is it the accelerator pedal that makes the car go forward?"

"I have worked out the brake makes it stop."

"I notice you use both clutch and brake at the same time, why is that?"

"Is it to stop the car equally, applying the brakes evenly on both sides of the car?"

"Is...."

"SHUT UP, with all the questions" Tony shouted. "I am trying to get us home in one piece, now is not the time to be teacher's pet and ask so many questions."

The Count looked at Tony and quietly laughed to himself, as Tony was looking rather flustered.

Exiting the parameter of Southampton, Tony changed down from 4th to 3rd gear. As he did he struggled to gauge it correctly, which caused the gears to fiercely grate.

"Come on, Come on Tony, pull it together, you can do this." He muttered.

Locating 3rd correctly he pressed down hard on the accelerator, powering the car forward. The note of the engine sang as the engine revs increased, similar to that of a violin practising prior to a concerto.

Tony checked his rear view mirror as the interior of the car flashed with an intermittent blue light.

"Shit, we've been pulled. That's fucked it." Tony said.

"Why are we slowing?" the Count asked

"If we don't pull over we will be all over the radios and every copper in the South will be looking for us."

"Hmmm" the Count pondered, not convinced this was the best strategy.

"Ok Nigel Mansell, could you please step out of the car." The police officer asked.

"Yes certainly officer, what seems to be the problem?" Tony replied trying his best to pronounce his words correctly without slurring.

"By the smell of your breath Sir, it is obvious you have been drinking. Would you please escort me to the back of the squad car and aahh!" The Policeman's voice initially calm turned to a loud scream.

Tony jolted his head back slightly as he witnessed the Policeman being lifted clean off the ground. The Count from behind had thrust his hand through the Policeman's back and exited his chest. The Counts hand burst out from the Policeman's uniform holding his beating heart. Quickly retreating his arm back in the direction of which it came, the Policeman fell to the ground without a murmur. Twitching and heavily bleeding the Policeman was no longer a concern.

"Man what is wrong with you, Police always travel in two's the other officer is probably on the radio right now!" Tony yelled at the Count.

Without saying a word the count removed his blood soaked shirt and threw it on the ground. Getting back in the car the Count patiently waited for Tony to drive.

Tony looked at the Police Volvo and shook his head in disbelief, as he realised the other Policeman's head was not just resting on the steering wheel, he too were dead.

Chapter Twelve

Carl had been looking forward to his monthly night out with the lads since his hangover had cleared from lasts month's night out. Carl being twenty-eight and married had made a pact to meet up with four of his single long- term friends once a month. Walking out of his three-bed semi onto the pavement, he headed in the direction of the bar where they were all meeting. He was very well groomed; he liked to think that although he was married he still might turn a few ladies' heads. Looking at his watch, he noticed that he was running slightly late and picked up his pace.

Arriving at the venue he noticed his mates were already standing at the bar.

"Sorry boys, a little bit late. Whose round is it?"

One of his friends answered,

"Yours, we've been waiting ages for you to get them in, the things you do to avoid buying a pint!"

Getting into the flow of the evening and several pints later, Carl noticed that he had an admirer. Every time he looked over to his admirer she looked back at Carl with seductive eyes. Being so obvious, Carl turned and looked over his shoulder to check that there wasn't a hunk of a man standing behind him. It appeared all clear, only his buddies, so it couldn't be them attracting her attention. Leaning into one of his buddies he asked,

"See that chick over there? The one built for pleasure. Look I think she is definitely giving me fuck eyes!"

His friend observed and monitored the lady for a while and leant into Carl and said,

"For sure, you old hound. Married and still got the magic."

Carl looked at the lady again, as he did she got up and slowly, sexily walked over to him. Her eyes locked on target, she came right up to him and placed both hands on his chest and pressed her firm bosoms against him. Looking up at him she asked,

"Do you want to shake this place and have some fun?"

Carl, a man who strongly believed in not paying for sex, asked,

"You look fine to me but I am married and have a lot to risk and I don't do hookers." Not insulted by this or fazed she replied,

"I won't be telling anyone and I don't charge!"

Very rusty at playing the field, Carl felt a little nervous and quickly thought through his options. He could go have some fun with a fine hottie, return and have a few more beers with the lads or he could just stay with the lads. The decision suddenly became easy for him and he acknowledged to the lass that all systems were go.

Turning towards the boys, Carl cockily said,

"Guys won't be too long, keep mine on ice. Be back in a bit."

Between the friends they made obvious jokes about him not taking long at all, as he escorted the lady out of the venue.

Holding the lady's hand, she guided Carl to the rear car park. Bleeping her remote, it became obvious which car was hers. Carl got into the passenger's seat and asked,

"Where are we going? I thought we could have a little fun in the alley or something."

"Here will be fine, the forecast is rain."

Stretching out his legs and getting a little more comfortable, the lady leant over and gently kissed his neck. Moving towards his lips she engaged in a deep passionate kiss. Whilst kissing, she massaged his balls with her hand, stimulating him to a semi hard erection. Undoing his zip she moved her head down into his lap, whilst taking his penis out and slowly caressing it. Taking it into her mouth, she slowly bobbed up and down making his penis fully hard. Placing his hands on her head, he moved her blonde hair so he could watch her perform this kind act.

"Hey look at me whilst you're doing me." He asked softly.

She looked up at him with sexy eyes, which he found very stimulating, until her eyes turned. Glowing white with a tinge of cat like yellow, she sank her fangs into his main vein. Drinking hard and fast she snarled, using her left hand she pinned Carl to the seat.

"Fuuuuckkkkk, ahhhhhhhh, get off, get off, you psycho!"

Carl tried to summon the strength to pull her head off of his manhood but he felt weak and was going into shock. The twitching of his body indicated to the lady he was empty, releasing her bite she sat back upright in the driver's seat.

Placing a hooked chord on the door handle of the passenger's door she then started the car. Driving carefully, not to attract any attention, she drove until she entered a dark back road which had grass verges on the near side. Pulling the chord, the door popped open; with a stiff shove she pushed Carl out of the moving car.

"Told you I wouldn't tell!" The lady uttered as she leant across to pull the door shut.

Vicky closed her eyes in hope it would stop the world spinning. Celebrating her friend's 30th Birthday, the group had decided to end the evening by consuming vast quantities of tequila. As the taxi she was sitting in went left, she found herself being flung to the right. The taxi driver keen to make the destination was mindful that he didn't want her being ill in his cab. He occasionally looked at her in the mirror and wondered why young women get in such a state and thought of his daughter who was twenty-three.

Stopping outside her house, the cabby looked at Vicky and shouted to wake her,

"Hi Darling, you are home now, that's £9.12 please."

Stirring and fighting back being ill, Vicky fumbled in her bag for her purse. Dropping her mobile phone and house keys she located her purse.

"Here keep the change." She replied as she gave him a ten- pound note.

"Thanks, please do take care, it's a bad old world out there." He advised in a fatherly voice.

Closing the taxi door she stumbled forward, trying to replace her phone into her handbag.

Losing her balance for a second she stumbled left straight into a lamp post.

"Hello Mr Lamp post, how are you tonight? Thanks for your support; you are always here for me aren't you?" She rambled, which could just be heard over the sound of the taxi pulling away.

Fumbling with her keys she held them close to her face, trying to establish which one was the front door key. Taking a long blink she tried hard to focus,

"Shit!" she uttered as she saw the keys fall in slow motion to the floor.

Keeping one hand on the lamp post, she bent down, her head was spinning so fast she thought she was actually dancing with the lamp post. Extending her fingers she located the keys and picked them up. Just as she did, a pair of large shoes appeared at the spot where the keys were. Without standing, she raised her head to follow the figure up to his face.

"Hi, dropped my keys!" she nervously explained.

Offering his hand to help her up, Vicky grabbed it and pulled to get back to her feet.

"Thanks."

"My pleasure." The man replied as his fangs extended down and his face turned.

Although Vicky was very drunk and was struggling to make out the man's detail, a natural instinct told her she was in trouble.

Taking both hands, the man dragged her to a nearby parked car. Turning her, he threw her hands onto the roof of the Ford Focus, whilst upping her short skirt.

With one hand holding her head sideways onto the roof, he used the other to get his penis out and ripped her knickers off. Kicking her legs slightly to widen her stance he forced himself upon her.

His hand that held her in place moved slightly to cover her mouth, whilst he pumped away from behind. Releasing his fertile fluid into her he lunged down onto her neck, sinking his fangs deep into her bloodstream. Drinking just enough he released his bite, he took his hand off her face and stood tall. Shaking his penis a couple of times before placing it back into his trousers, he looked around him to ensure he had not been seen. Taking big strides he sped off, walking fast but without breaking into a jog. He briefly looked over his shoulder at Vicky, who was sat in a heap against the car, holding her head sobbing loudly.

Wiping his brow, Chris had decided to stop dancing and take a break. Walking from the dance floor towards the other lads, the music changed and moved to a slow record.

The DJ announced that the night was nearly over and the last ten minutes would be the last chance to make a move. Not sure about the Erection Section as the DJ named it, Chris carried on walking.

Nearly at the edge of the dance floor a young attractive woman stepped in his way and asked,

"Would you like to dance?"

Taking a moment to look her up and down, pleased with what he saw he answered,

"Why not, if it will make your night."

Breaking into a contagious smile, the lady did not reply and took Chris's hand.

Finding a spot on the dance floor they adopted the usual slow dance positions. Bobbing from one side to the other, they slowly moved in a circle. The lady nested into Chris's strapping frame and let off a polite sigh of content. As she positioned her crutch in his groin area, Chris was unsure if to make a move or not. Briefly looking down he noticed her big, blue, infectious eyes beaming up at him. Hesitating he stopped his head from going in for the kiss, as the record playing ended and the next slow track started. Before he could pluck up the courage, he felt her placing delicate pecks on his neck. Smiling he pulled her in closer to his body to put some expression into his action, when she sank her fangs into him. Letting off a short whimper his attack went unnoticed, drowned out by the volume of the music. As she fed, she started to support his weight, as he became heavier and more lifeless she slowly dragged him to the other side of the dance floor. Totally fed she removed her bite, propping him up against a JBL speaker. Checking he did not fall over, she left him there and casually left the nightclub.

Paul looked around the empty train and wondered why people discarded their chewing gum on the window seal. He was on the last train out of Waterloo, heading for Farnborough Main. He had roughly counted about six people in his carriage, four behind him and two in seats opposite. Placing his headphones into his ears, he pressed play on his IPod. Although he had stayed uptown after work for a few drinks with colleagues, he was not too drunk. As the train jigged him around in his seat, he tried to align this movement to the beat of the track playing on his IPod. Singing out loud occasionally to the track he forgot there was other passengers on the train.

Stopping at Surbiton, two passengers left the carriage. Paul had noticed that one of the passengers opposite was a very attractive lady. As the journey continued he tried not to get caught looking at her long legs. It appeared that he was not very good at this game, as every time he took a sneaky look, she caught him. Stopping at Weybridge and Brookwood the carriage only accommodated the lady and Paul.

Looking up at the lady for another sneaky peak, he noticed she was staring hard at him. Feeling a little embarrassed he quickly diverted his eyes momentarily, before returning to look at her again. This time she extended her arm and made a come here gesture with her index finger. Turning to check this was definitely directed at him he put his finger on his own chest and mouthed "Me?"

Nodding, the lady moved over on her seat making room for Paul. Paul nearly at Farnborough thought he might be able to get a quick snog and hurried over to her. The train's motion made him loose his balance on route, as it jigged on the tracks, nearly falling straight on top of her; he managed to regain his cool by catching a handrail. Sitting down smoothly next to her, he was just about to ask her name when the lady lunged forward, pulling him towards her. Taking a big bite she locked onto his neck, before the pain became too much Paul repeatedly punched her in her abdomen, trying to get her to release. With no effect from his short- range blows, he felt the sensation of his inner strength being removed and became tired, exhaling loudly, he slowly passed away.

Chapter Thirteen

Melinda sat exhausted, now with a family of eight to look after; she was quite pleased Leon, Michael and Jason had all flown the nest. She couldn't help think of the magnitude of the population now, understanding she was one of many that the Count regularly impregnated. She was also delighted that after the last delivery, Antonio, the Count never came to renew his membership. She didn't wish to either question why or even think too hard about it, just in case the Count picked up on her thoughts and be reminded.

The thought that the process would be over as soon as Antonio flew the nest, was all that was keeping her going. Reaching for the remote she changed the channel of the TV, she was bored of watching a show called 'Big Brother' and wanted an update on what was going on in the real world.

The news was nearly the same every day, multiple stabbings, shootings and other murders, which the Police could not understand. Melinda understood that these events were all cover up's for Vampire attacks. The Police could not really release their concerns of the nature of the many killings. The census of opinion across the nation was it was no longer safe to go out at night and many people admitted they didn't feel safe to go out alone and that the Police were no longer respected. The Police admitted that they were bogged down with paperwork and were looking into new methods to free them up, to increase Police presence.

Luckily for the Count, the news of record all time high petrol prices and soaring inflation, outshone the increase of killings. A worldwide credit crunch was affecting the world economy, forcing house prices to dramatically fall month after month after month. Feeling the doom and gloom with the rest of the nation, her viewing was interrupted by the Count entering her thoughts telepathically,

'Melinda, thank you for your assistance in achieving the goal of self existence, my work is now done in this Country. I enjoyed our intimacy and hope you can forgive me for turning you and making your world the lonely one you now understand.'

As his thoughts faded from her mind, she could not help start to miss him and feel that she could never love again. It is a problem when everyone you meet, ends up being your dinner, it cramps your love life somewhat. She also thought she could not risk trusting anyone to reveal her true identity, it would be asking quite a lot to ask your partner to accept your nightly activities. Looking at her watch, she knew she would soon have to go out food shopping. With both hands she ran her fingers through her hair, sinking her head down whilst taking a deep breath.

Flicking the TV channels, she surfed until she stopped on a documentary about migrating to Australia. She liked the idea of making a new start once the kids had all flown the nest and pondered on what the Count had said.

'This Country? What stops me jumping on a flight and starting a new life with fresh pickings in another Country?'

The more she thought about the idea the more she liked it, until she felt the cold air of the Count, on her neck. He had materialised, holding a man who was white with fear and physically shaking from head to foot. Thrusting the man forward to Melinda the Count said in a jovial voice,

"I brought you a takeaway!"

The man left cowering in the middle of the room, looked at Melinda fearing what was coming next. Melinda didn't take her strike immediately and looked at the Count with affectionate eyes,

"Thank you, I didn't fancy eating out tonight!"

Melinda looked at the Count, a handsome man with great power and realised that she was actually in love with him.

Taking the opportunity as his predators looked at each other lovingly, the man ran for the door. Taking no more than six strides the Count zoomed across the room blocking the door.

"Where do you think you are going?" the count asked, as he grabbed the man by the scruff.

Unable to speak, the man stood lower than his normal posture, he shook knowing his time was up. Turning the man the Count said,

"He is all yours, take him."

Without delay, Melinda shot forward her teeth bared and mouth wide open. The man closed his eyes, knowing this was his last few moments of existence and awaited his fate.

Locking onto his neck, she looked over the man's shoulder, acknowledging to her offspring it was safe to feed. Like piranhas they darted out from their dark hiding places locking onto his naked arms, quickly finding his lifeline veins. As they drained the man, the Count held him firmly in place. Whilst drinking the man's blood, Melinda looked up from his neck and rolled her eyes with content before giving a flirtatious stare to the Count. Removing her bite from the man, Melinda moved forward towards the Count. Engaging in a passionate kiss they shared the last of the man's blood as they exchanged it between their kiss. Pulling away from the Count Melinda asked,

"Make love to me."

Releasing his grip on the man, the Count moved towards Melinda embracing her,

"I thought you would never ask." he replied, as they engulfed their faces into another passionate kiss.

The man slowly fell to the floor, hugging the wall, twitching slightly as he rested in a collapsed heap. Melinda's kids followed him to the floor, without releasing their bites. Although no blood was left they found it fun to practice their vice locking bites.

Picking Melinda up the Count made his way to the bedroom, caressing her with soft and passionate kisses as he walked. Placing her on her bed he removed her denim mini skirt, lifting her bottom up off of the bed to allow the skirt to gracefully glide over her bronze long legs. Shortly followed by her white G-string the Count moved up her legs kissing gently as he moved towards her naked vagina. Placing his nose in between her vagina lips he slowly nested it before placing a wet kiss directly on her clitoris. Taking his hands he warmly caressed the contours of Melinda's finely shaped abdomen. Gyrating her midriff in motion with his tongue, he pleasured her just long enough and pulled away before she could climax. Moving up her body he gently fondled her firm breasts licking her nipples vibrantly with the end of his tongue. Melinda had already taken her upper clothes off and started to help the Count remove his clothing. Locking in a deep kiss, Melinda suddenly thought although she really wanted this to happen she did not wish to become pregnant again.

Kissing his chiselled body, the Count removed his trousers and underwear. Returning to missionary position the Count gently entered her. Slowly thrusting his penis in and out of her in a long and sensual rhythm, he pulled her head from the pillow. Placing his hand behind her shoulder blades he lifted her up, thrusting his penis in deeper than she believed it could go. Holding this position he grinded his pubic bone on her clitoris. Using his defined back muscles to maintain this position, he took his other hand and gently clasped her jaw line. Opening her mouth as she climaxed he inserted his index finger in her mouth, with little force he stroked her tongue.

Whispering in her ear the Count romantically said,

"Over the many thousands of years, I have loved many times. I have never loved anyone as I do you;

please remember this moment, me for all your remaining years."

Shuddering from her multiple climaxes, she included a nod to indicate yes as her answer.

Slowly pulling out from her, the Count lowered her back to the mattress, placing a soft and moist kiss on her forehead. Placed his forefinger on her pouting lips, he silently mouthed shh and then lifted his finger to his own lips. Placing a kiss on his index finger, he replaced his finger back onto Melinda's lips.

"I have to go, one day I will return for good I hope, keep me in your thoughts."

Dazed by the moment, Melinda took her time to answer; before the words could leave her lips the Count had teleported out of the room.

Chapter Fourteen

Enjoying his weekend, Tony felt the need to relax and distance himself a bit from the Count. Sat with his feet up, Tony had located himself in the entertainments room and had decided to play on the Xbox games console. Changing from Megatron into a car, he leaned to the left in the same direction as the car travelled on the screen. Rapidly pressing the fire button the car shot laser blasts, destroying the Police car and station in its path.
"Yes have it!"

Pressing the pause button, Tony looked round as he had felt the Count's presence.

"Tony I understand you wish to blow things up and relive your youth but I have some serious matters, I wish to discuss with you."

"Oki doki, what's on your mind?" Tony replied whilst, exiting and turning off the games console.

"My work here is done, I now require to relocate to China, their population is currently around 1,321,851,888."

Tony knew that this was not going to be a light conversation and headed towards the beer fridge in the Kitchen.

"That seems a pretty accurate number there Vamps. Have you been doing your homework?" Tony asked as he made his way towards the kitchen.

Looking at Tony slightly puzzled almost astonished he would ask such a question he replied.

"Tony I do not study, I just know, do you disbelieve me?"

"Hey Vamps don't get all bent out of shape, I was only messing around with you, I am sure you don't want to argue about if you are a couple out with your approximate guess. Anyway what has brought all this on anyway?"

Pouring a can of lager, Tony bobbed his head from side to side mouthing 'One billion and three million' in a mother hen action. When the Count firmly responded,

"Enough! I need you to close Life Savers and move out of here urgently. I am happy to split the profits of the business with you 50/50. I require your assistance with the migration, once I am set up in China you are free to do as you please."

"Hey man, firstly I don't speak Chinese and secondly I don't really want to go."

"Tony, you will not be coming."

Taking a large swig of his drink, he looked at the Count with a facial expression insinuating that the Count could not possibly do this on his own.

"Well if you insist and you are sure you don't need me, I could use a holiday." Tony's thoughts were very much focused on half of more money than he could imagine in his wildest dreams.

"When are you thinking of moving?" Tony timidly asked.

Pulling a stool and sitting at the kitchen Island, the Count placed his finger on his chin and fondled it in a circular motion.

"I wish to be ready within a week."

Spitting the contents of his lager in a wide and fine spray, Tony briefly choked.

"Are you mad? We have clients fully booked for the next six months at least. It is pretty sick to build up the hopes of those people and then kick them in the nuts further still. Oh sorry you're on your own now."

"Tony I understand you are passionate about your brainchild but all good things have to come to an end. You didn't believe we could carry on doing this for ever did you? I needed our population to get to a sufficient number to guarantee self existence. I now need you to look after the family and especially Melinda. I am very fond of her and I ask of you to guard her with your life."

Tony knowing he really did not have any choice in all of this, scratched his nose and used his thumb to scratch the inside of his right nostril. Moving his hand over his face he paused before gradually pulling it down over his face. Taking a deep breath he moved opposite and sat down.

"So let me get this straight, I wind the business up, get you to China, then I am free to be me, well except keep an eye on things etc."

"In your simple terms yes, Tony." The Count replied in a reassuring tone.

Taking a few more seconds to process the Counts offer, Tony stood up took a large swig of his drink and said,

"I am in, on one condition."

"Enlighten me, Tony."

"You can tell Lucy, she is going to have to phone up all the clients and cancel their appointments."

"Consider it done." Replied the Count feeling they had again made a human promise.

Monday morning came round quickly. Tony was up extra early and made sure he was prepared for Lucy. Leaning back in his leather chair he nervously rearranged items on his desk. With the imminent change in direction of the business he had decided to dress very casual in blue Jeans and a grey v-neck T-shirt. Looking at his watch it was 5 minutes before Lucy normally arrived. Thinking to himself he couldn't help feel that the Count was going to tuck him up. An alarm beeped repeatedly for 10 seconds, indicating the parameter gates were open, which meant Lucy would soon be upon the manor.

"Fucking Wanker! I knew he would shaft me." He rambled under his breath.

"I hope you are not referring to me?" the count said in a commanding manner.

"I thought you had bailed on me!" Tony nervously replied

"We had a promise; I said I would deal with the situation and that I will."

Suddenly, Tony realised that letting the Count deal with breaking the news, was probably not such a good idea.

"Be gentle with her mate, don't do your usual, I'm fucking off to China so it all ends now. Please be a little creative."

"Oh Tony, after all this time, I think you really don't get me at all."

Breaking their conversation, the sound of Lucy's car door slamming made them focus on the task in hand. The Count boldly moved forwards into the reception area and awaited Lucy. For the real first time he thought about playing a joke on Tony, making it utterly dreadful for Lucy, just to see the look on his face. As he thought this, he realised he was becoming more human than originally hoped and also realised how much he valued Tony highly as a soul mate.

Bounding into the room in her usual manner Lucy took off her coat and hung it up.

"Who's for coffee? Wow what a weekend I have had."

Changing the filter of the coffee machine and refilling the coffee, did not phase her conversation,

"I met a man Friday night, he's gorgeous, we talked all evening and well, we didn't see much of Saturday & Sunday, if you know what I mean!"

The Count, trying to get a word in edge ways paused and looked at Tony, with a facial expression of concern.

Understanding what was being asked of him, Tony looked at Lucy to check for the glow. Looking back at the Count, Tony shook his head providing her with the all clear.

Taking a deep breath the Count collated his thoughts, when Lucy fired more conversation at them.

"Don't think I'm being slutty or anything I don't usually leap into bed with the first man I see. I don't mind telling you guys that I have been hung out to dry for the last six months. Oh he was wonderful, a gentleman, a laugh and a good F...." Remembering where she was and who she was talking to, she decided not to finish her sentence and looked up from her coffee.

"Lucy please sit down, I have some news that I need to tell you before you start." The Count firmly said.

"Am I in trouble?"

"No, we are more than delighted with you and your loyalty. What I am about to say has nothing to do with your commitment to the Company."

Lucy leant forward on her chair and rested her chin on her hands showing an inquisitive nature. The Count continued to explain,

"Although we have had excellent results with our practice, the Governing bodies will not accept our methods and have enforced closure. We obviously do not wish to get in any form of trouble and will have to adopt the normal practice and register our methods. To get full approval and jump through all the necessary hoops, will set us back about four years."

Not entirely sure what impact this news meant to her, she automatically asked,

"So does this mean I'm getting the sack?"

Smiling and straightening his already strong posture the Count replied,

"No not at all, we have discussed in detail and decided to ask you to work one more week for us and in return we will give you two years salary, cash. I hope this is acceptable to you?"

Taking no longer than about two seconds Lucy replied,

"Heck yeah, met a dream guy, get a huge bonus, well I might just try my luck a bit further and put the lottery on this Wednesday."

"Tony if you would like to explain the proceedings from here to Lucy, I have other business to attend to." The count commanded, as he walked out of the reception area.

Tony explained the finer details of Lucy's involvement and shuddered at what he had to achieve in the set week.

"Ok if you can cancel all appointments from tomorrow onwards, we will of course see today's clients."

Tony made his way into the back office to find the count. Understanding that he would need to feed he expected to find the Count sat in behind the desk as normal.

Surprised the office was empty Tony ventured off around the Manor to find him.

Finally arriving in the kitchen, he had not found the Count. Shaking his head he realised that he would have to tell today's clients face to face that they were not getting cured today.

Rubbing his hand over his head he knew the first client would be waiting in reception, it was not something he could put off any longer.

Walking into the reception boldly he advanced to Mr Simmonds,

"Hello sir, I have some very bad news, we have had a very serious technical fault with our systems. We are not going to be able to treat you, I am so sorry."

Mr Simmonds face dropped, it was not bad enough that he had such a horrible disease; he had tasted being cured and now knew it would slowly and painfully kill him. In a frail and desperate voice, Mr Simmonds looked up at Tony and said,

"I can pay a little more if it will help."

His eyes were filled with his last hope; he fumbled in his inner jacket pocket to find his cheque book.

Slowly moving forward to Mr Simmonds, Tony reached out holding the man's arm stopping him taking his cheque book from his pocket. Looking at Mr Simmonds straight in the eye, Tony's face bursting with true compassion said,

"I am SO sorry it is not about money, we cannot risk treating you. The chance of you not surviving the treatment is far too high. For this reason we have been ordered to close the service. If I could do something right now, trust me I would."

Taking Mr Simmonds hand, Tony clasped it with both of his. The sound of Lucy sucking up a tear broke the moment.

Mr Simmonds slowly turned without saying a word and shuffled towards the door. Tony stood motionless, hands by his side and watched a broken man leave the reception.

Taking a deep breath and fighting back a big lump in his throat Tony looked at Lucy. Lucy understanding that Tony was well out of his comfort zone, stood and opened her arms,

"Come here you poor sausage."

Tony welcomed her invitation and accepted her kind offer. Resting his chin on her head he shut his eyes and composed himself.

"Just think of all the people you have helped, you can't save them all!" Lucy reassured.

Tony gently shook his head on hers, this was the first time he had really thought about what the business was actually doing to people. Tony suddenly felt awful about himself and uttered under his breath,

"If only you knew the half of it."

Separating from their team hug, Tony briefly looked at Lucy and wondered for a second if there was any chemistry between them. Snapping out of this thought he said,

"One down seven to go. I am going to need a stiff drink tonight, I am sure."

Systematically, Tony broke the terrible news to the other seven, destroying their worlds. Tony felt like crap about the whole situation and for the first real time he resented the Count and all he stood for. Looking at Lucy in tears on the phone as she told yet another client their lives were also shattered. He realised that he was dwelling in his own self pity and decided to offer some form of comfort to Lucy. Standing behind her as she finished her final call for the day, he put his hands on her shoulders and calmly said,

"I am so sorry I got you involved in such a soul destroying job."

Lucy placed the handset back in its cradle and placed her right hand on Tony's hand, which was on her left shoulder. Gently squeezing his hand she said nothing and pushed her chair backwards ready to stand. Turning to Tony, her face swollen with sadness, she placed her bottom lip over her top one and took a long blink.

Picking her handbag up, she moved out from behind her desk,

"See you tomorrow." She said in a quivery voice, as she left the manor.

Tony had a strange feeling he would never see Lucy again.

Lucy did return the next day and the next and the next, the week passed fast. Tony still had a few things to attend to but on the whole was winning.

Lucy had called every client on the waiting list and given them the bad news. Winding up her last call Lucy looked at her watch and noted she had four hours to go. Leaning back in her chair she crossed her legs and closed her eyes for a moment. Rubbing her left eye she felt knackered and was not too bothered if she never saw this office again. As she rubbed her right eye Tony entered the room,

"How is it going? All done?"

"Yes finally, that was tough."

"That is excellent, I really do appreciate you doing this for us, I was not sure if you were going to come back Tuesday."

"To be honest I did think twice about calling in but you guys have been so good to me and I would kick myself if I jeopardised two years salary."

"Oh shit. I didn't get chance to go to the bank, I am really sorry, would a cheque be ok?" Tony enquired.

Slowly standing Lucy walked to Tony, she had a naughty glint in her eye.

"Of course it is." She said as she huddled in for a cuddle.

Wearing a tightly fitted skirt and her blouse showing a fair amount of cleavage, Tony was thinking naughty thoughts himself. He had always been attracted to her but had managed to maintain a professional relationship.

"You are such a nice bloke, I will miss you!" Lucy added,

Tony thought, 'don't blow it; she is just being a girly chick.'

As Lucy pulled away from her cuddle she looked at Tony with puppy dog eyes. Sensing Tony wasn't going to risk embarrassing himself she effortlessly advanced forward and placed a friendly kiss on his lips. Again not sure if this was a parting kiss or a 'thanks for everything' kind of kiss, Tony remained still not interacting, although he wanted to embrace her and passionately kiss her. Pulling away from him a little, Lucy asked,

"Where is Roberto?"

Feeling her breath on his lips as she spoke made him a little nervous. Taking a large gulp he replied,

"He's packing, why do you ask?"

Placing another kiss, she softly spoke,

"I would hate to be disturbed."

Now fully understanding that his luck was in, Tony moved forward and engaged in a passionate kiss. As they kissed Lucy made a muffled moaning sound which indicated to Tony she was enjoying the moment. Placing his arms around her he caressed her back, moving slightly apart he moved his right hand to Lucy's left breast. Softly feeling her plump breasts he felt her hand move down and stroke his semi hard penis.

Pulling away from the kiss to regain air, Lucy spoke in a whispery voice,

"I have always wanted you, even at my interview I found you very hot."

Picking her up, Tony moved towards the reception desk, clearing a space for Lucy's petite bottom as he placed her on the desk.

Hitching up her skirt, he parted her knickers to one side and proceeded to perform oral sex. Throwing her head back Lucy took a deep breath, opening her legs wider allowing Tony to work his magic. Placing her right hand on the back of his head she moved his head at the pace she liked. With her left hand she unfastened her blouse and cupped her left breast. Tweaking her nipple through her bra she climaxed,

"Oh Tony you're the daddy!"

Placing slow and moist kisses on her inner thighs, he waited for her to finish her orgasm. Confident she had finished, he gently pulled her forward off of the desk slightly. Taking his manhood from his trousers he tapped it on her clitoris before placing it in her. Holding her legs on the tops of her hold ups he started his rhythm. Fearing he would spoil the moment he felt he had to ask,

"Are you on the pill?"

In a seductive voice, she replied,

"No, don't worry I will swallow your juices."

Tony was already trying not to cum too quickly and with Lucy's offer it finished him off.

Quickly pulling out he tried not to ejaculate in her. Leaping from the desk, Lucy homed in on his penis like a heat seeking missile. Tony rolled his eyes in ecstasy, as Lucy covered his exploding hydrant with her mouth.

Placing his penis back into his underpants and doing his trousers up, Tony didn't quite know what to say.

'Thank you,' would sound a bit desperate and 'that was nice', would sound too demeaning. He decided to not comment on what had just happened and break the awkwardness with a light joke.

"I better get my cheque book, not for that of course, I mean for your severance pay." Making a complete 'dog's ear' of it, he blushed and made his way to his office.

With Lucy all paid up and all the clients informed Tony sat back in his office chair and pondered for a moment,

'It was good while it lasted' he knew he was going to miss being his own boss. Locking the door for the last time he picked up a box of files and made his way to the Kitchen. The Count was already sitting at the Kitchen Island, spinning a two pound coin on the granite surface to pass the time.

"It sounded like Lucy left on a good note!" the Count joked.

"Yeah, didn't see that one coming, well you know what I mean!"

Placing the box on a kitchen top, Tony ventured into the fridge for a beer. Talking with his head still in the American sized fridge he said,

"Right I have booked your flight, just let me have a bank account number when you are sorted and I will transfer your half over."

The Count did not reply and looked at Tony with a patient smirk.

"What?" Tony asked, pulling the ring pull of the beer can.

"Tony, why do I need flight tickets? It is not as if I even have a passport. I will be travelling 'Teleport Airways' as usual. I will contact you, once I have found your replacement, it is a shame you don't speak Chinese."

Although Tony didn't like the thought of him being surplus to requirements, he dwelled on being free, which pleased him more than upset him.

"Yeah shame, not!" He added as he took a swig of his lager.

The Count choosing to ignore Tony continued,

"I will need about £100K in cash though. If you could sort this for me I would appreciate it."

"Not a problem, are you out tonight? I am going to have an early one if that is ok with you?"

"Yes Tony, I am, I will be quiet on my return."

Tony picked his can up and moved towards the entertainment room and grunted,

"Cool."

Taking a moment Tony thought about what the Count had just said, turning he asked,

"If you usually Teleport around the world, why did I find you in a coffin and looking as if the rats had been eating your face?"

"I have been waiting for you to ask this question for a long time Tony. For my survival I need two companions, one being money and the second being my guardian. When I set off for England, electronic money transfers were not possible. With the money I knew I would need to survive long enough to populate England, I could not risk it being stolen. Not having any identification, meant I had to stow myself. I thought that no one in their right mind would open a coffin with blood vials surrounding it. I knew that if I waited long enough you would eventually find me."

Hurling his head back in astonishment absorbing what the Count had just said, Tony replied.
"What are you saying, waiting for me, are you sure? I was just the numbskull that got dragged into lifting the lid off!"
"No Tony, you are the chosen one for England. I have just located the chosen one for China. This is by far a bigger task; their population is very much out of control."
"Now if you will excuse me I am feeling a bit peckish." The Count added.
Tony acknowledged this with a methodical nod, turned and continued into the entertainment room.

Chapter Fifteen

Tony could not stop thinking, 'If I had only phoned in sick that day or something, this evil species would not be spreading like wild fire across the country.' Tony watched the TV but he was not really taking in the content. He could not get past the thought it was all his fault, Richard would still be living and so many people would not have lost their souls. He tried to balance his negativity with the positive thought of all of the people that have been cured of terminal diseases. Which quickly turned to a negative again as he thought, 'Spending an eternity of feeding off people's blood, may be worse than the prospect of actually dying.'

Thinking about the romp he had just had with Lucy, made him see a brief positive but again quickly his opinion changed to one of sheer guilt.

With the weight of the world on his shoulders, Tony repeatedly flicked up and down the TV channels, without really paying any attention to what was on.

Waking the next day, the TV was still on. Tony was hunched in the recliner chair, his posture mirroring the shape of the chair. He stretched his neck to relieve the crick from sleeping awkwardly. He tried to focus on the TV but his eyes were still very much sleepy. This time of the morning was the only time that Tony actually felt comfortable about himself. Within minutes of waking the reality of what he had caused hit him hard and grated against his decent morals.

"You dumb fuck!" he shouted to himself.

His guilt felt enormous, a pulsating bubble strong increasing in size with every breath. He felt he did not deserve to ever smile or enjoy himself ever again. Picking up a piece of cold pizza from his plate, which he must have fallen asleep eating last night, he took a large bite. Rubbing his left eye he pondered whilst he munched,

'How can I fix this?' Before he could summon any brain activity to this question he felt the Counts presence.

Looking up from the TV to acknowledge the Count he took another large bite.

"I hope you rested well? I didn't wish to wake you when I returned late last night."

"It's not as comfy as it looks this chair, you know."

The Count took a moment to interrogate Tony's thoughts, which for some reason he couldn't, then asked,

"Are you alright Tony? You seem distant."

"Got a lot on my mind, shall we say!" Tony sheepishly replied.

"As long as you are ok Tony, now, what do friends do when they say goodbye? Do they shake hands? I am new to this."

Putting the crust of his pizza down, Tony got up out of his chair and asked,

"Are you off then?"

"Yes Tony, I have much ahead of me to do in China. I can trust you to oversee here so there is no real reason for me to delay my mission any further."

Moving forward, the Count looked down at Tony for inspiration of what to do next.

"Ooh you make me feel so special. Well it's not like we can go and sink a few beers, grab a curry and send you off properly, so yeah I guess this is goodbye then."

Opening his arms he indicated for the Count to embrace him in a manly hug. As they firmly squeezed each other Tony said,

"You will be in touch with the bank details in your usual manner, I take it."

The Count thought for a moment and put a small distance between them and omitted.

"For some reason, I struggle to read your thoughts and fear that I may not be able to communicate with you telepathically. What other method do you suggest?"

Looking at the Count with a mixture of astonishment and relief, he moved towards the coffee table and scribbled his email address down.

"Here take this, give it to my counter partner and ask him to email me the bank details."

"Ok Tony, take care of Melinda and yourself." Before Tony could answer the Count disappeared into thin air.

Feeling a huge wave of relief, Tony stretched in the spot where he stood and rubbed his face hard with both hands. Almost as if he felt dirty cuddling the Count, he then scratched his arm just above his elbow.

"Right, let's get this place all packed up and transfer a bucket load of money into my account."

The thought of many millions of pounds at his disposal, distracted him from his previous overwhelming guilt.

He also thought he might take the opportunity to move nearer to his parent's location, about forty miles from the manor, a town called Camberley. He had done as the Count had asked and slowly distanced himself from friends and family, but felt he needed to see a little more of his folks as he hugely missed them.

Working furiously all weekend, Tony managed to complete the tasks in hand. He felt comfortable he was in a position to move quickly, when the time was correct.

Driving to Camberley on the following Monday, he visited over eight estate agents. He was getting very bored of going over the same information at each agent;

5 bed detached, drive/garage, off road gated access, short chain and no mortgage will be required.

He wished he had not packed the entertainment room away and would have preferred to perform the repeated qualifying questions and interrogation from each agent online. Tony had decided to move all of his personal items into storage and move into a delightful five star hotel, just minutes out of Camberley, whilst he searched for his new home.

Although his position of wealth and free time would be the envy of most. He realised that the last few years of absolute madness had changed him from a lazy, deadbeat to a high pressure go getter. Sitting in a cafe in town, he fidgeted with an empty sugar tube. He pondered on the fact that he was going to outlive all his friends and family, he understood why the Count was so lonely. Observing the many different people in the cafe all infatuated with their own life, he decided he needed something to occupy his time and stimulate his mind. By the time he had finished his coffee, he left the cafe none the wiser about his master plan.

Stopping at the entrance of the cafe, he deliberated on which way to turn. For the first time in a long time he had nothing pressing to do. As he made the decision to walk into the town centre, his mobile phone rang. In a confident executive voice he answered,

"Hi, you're speaking with Tony."

The caller being an Estate Agent, explaining that they had the perfect house for him and he needed to view it urgently. This sounded ideal as he was mindful he wanted to set up the PC and not miss the Counts email. He did not want the count popping over for any reason whatsoever. He really hoped he would never see the Count again. Confirming he could view the property in an hour he terminated the call. He was going to view a six bed, which an elderly lady previously owned but unfortunately, had recently passed away. Tony couldn't help wonder if her death was natural, or caused by one of the Counts clan. This thought reminded Tony that if so it was all his fault.

Pulling up to the gates of the property, he gave a polite honk of the Astons horn. A few moments passed, as the Estate Agent worked out how to open the gates. Driving in to the property grounds slowly and considerately, the Estate Agent waited eagerly. Her face alight with excitement, Tony's Aston Martin provided the impression that he was serious and had the money behind him to go forward. As Tony got out of his car she shut her eyes temporarily and thought of the commission.

"Hello Mr Sherman, thank you for coming at such short notice. I think you will find you are not wasting your time."

As the Estate Agent went in to full pitch, Tony filtered her out and took in the detail of the impressive property. It was of course no comparison to the Manor but not a bad pad for a young, thirty year old bachelor. The property was about 25% below market value, as a recession loomed and the executors to the will wanted to quickly close this chapter of their life. Impressed with the property based in the 'posh end' of Camberley which ticked every box, Tony confirmed he would take it.

Even though there was no onward chain, the sale still took five weeks to complete before Tony could move in. In this five week period, Tony had religiously logged onto his email via a quaint little Internet cafe daily. He was surprised that he had not heard from the Count and felt a little bit worried if he was ok.

With all his items out of storage and nearly all unpacked, Tony used a Stanley knife to cut the packing strap securing his PC box tightly shut. Excited about building his little command centre again he boldly took a swipe with the knife,

"Bugger!" he shouted, as the blade passed through his Armani jeans and made a precision cut in his thigh. Watching a steady stream of blood form on his jeans, he waited for a moment. As quickly as the blood had appeared, the stream dried up and his cut had healed.

Man's Natural Predator

Tony had forgotten about his immortality and didn't like the reminder that he was not pure human.

Using lounge area two Tony hooked up his technology centre, ensuring all speakers and monitors were correctly placed for maximum audio and visual impact.

Pressing the 'on' button of his powerful PC, monitor one sprang to life. As the PC booted up, he somehow knew the email he was awaiting would be sitting in his inbox.

Surprised that there was only junk mail in his Inbox, he pressed the send and receive icon. Watching the task bar to see if there were any messages downloading, it read 50% then 100%. The normal 'bing bong' to notify of new mail made Tony shudder as he looked at the senders address.

The email read:

Hi Tony, Vamps here. I am really impressed with this email system. Using this will really free my mind up from the constant voices in my head. Not sure how I will get an email address as I feed but you have taught me many things are possible if you put your mind to it. Anyway here are the bank details as promised, please reply to this email to let me know when you have made the transfer. Bye for now.

Understanding that this was the only real tie to the Count, Tony decided to perform the transfer there and then. Transferring multiple millions of pounds out of the country would certainly be tracked by the likes of Custom & Excise, fraud investigators and even MI5. Tony had to be sure his audit trail was squeaky clean, entering a reference of Pharmaceutical Research. Tony hoped it would not attract too much attention.

Replying to the Counts email, Tony felt a sense of relief as this should be the last he would see or hear of the Count. Although he no longer had any real close friends he felt like a party was in order.

Visiting his new local pub he sat at the bar and supped a pint of high strength lager. As a matter of habit, Tony looked around to see if anyone was glowing before he could fully relax. Tapping his finger to the beat of an R&B track, he felt he was himself, not scared of being ripped apart, or saying the wrong thing. His moment of self indulgence was disturbed by a fellow drinker who plonked himself in the seat next to him.

"Alright?" the man asked.

"Yes thanks, to be fair really good."

"Well, someone having a good day! I am knackered, just done an hour's Karate lesson, I'm not eighteen anymore." The man explained.

Tony nodded although not really interested in sparking up a full blown conversation with the man.

Tony thought,

'Karate, I could get into that. This would use a lot of my time up and be mentally and physically demanding.'

Finishing the dregs of his pint, Tony excused himself to the man and left fuelled with the idea of becoming a Jedi type martial artist.

Tony spent hours trawling through websites, learning the many types of martial arts and understanding what they all had to offer. Tony made his mind up that he wished to follow and study the art of Ninjutsu. He found an organisation that offered a full time training course in the form of a boot camp, based in Japan. This entailed living a simple life and learning the true ways of the Ninja art form. The course enrolment fee of £5,000 did not faze Tony and with a start date in two week's time, Tony excitedly booked it.

Several days later as Tony was driving to his parents house, he thought,

'Am I fit enough to take on a new life as a Ninja?'

Changing down into third gear his thoughts were broken by the petrol light coming on. Even though Tony was absolutely minted the price of petrol was at an all time high. It was not the actual price that bothered Tony it was the fact that 70% of the price was duty. The government blamed the high price of the barrel and other issues but the truth is that it was a far too important revenue stream, which they were not willing to sacrifice.

Pulling up at his parent's home, he blipped the throttle as he switched off the engine. Letting his parent's and everyone several houses away from his parent's house know he had arrived.

As he shut the car door, Tony stood tall stretching his back and walked proudly to his parent's gate. He liked to think that his Mum and Dad were proud of him and maybe bragged slightly to their neighbours about his success. Closing the gate behind him he looked at the lounge window, where his mum normally peeped out just past the net curtains, to check who was coming to the front door.

Giving the front door his usual knock, Tony placed the front door key in. For some reason even though he had a spare key, he always knocked as he didn't want the mental image of catching them doing naughty stuff.

"Only me!" He shouted as he opened the door and boldly walked in. A little surprised with no reply, he thought they must be in the garden. He recalled when parking up he remembered seeing their car in the drive. As they were keen gardeners he walked past the lounge and straight to the kitchen, to use the back door. Grasping the door handle tight he used the correct amount of force to open it. To his surprise the handle didn't move and was locked from the inside. Taking a moment to look around the kitchen Tony began to fear for the worst. His mum was very particular about keeping a tidy ship and would not feel comfortable if dust existed on her surfaces. Tony noticed a coffee cup in the sink, which had a new breed of mould growing in the bottom of it.

"Mum, Dad, are you home?" Tony shouted, as he walked quickly to the lounge. As he got near to the lounge door, he got a waft of a very unpleasant smell, which Tony recognised to be death.

Opening the door forcefully, nearly taking it clean off its hinges, Tony froze where he stood. His pupils opened wide with disbelief, his mouth dropped open, his facial expression became vacant of any personality. Not breathing for nearly a minute, Tony took a big gasp and tried to process what he saw. His mum lay back in the sofa, her head resting on the top of the back cushion. Her mouth locked in a wide open position, indicating a painful period prior to dying. Her body was rapidly decaying, it was obvious that she had no fluid left. Her skin although old, was visibly loose around her arms, Tony knew what had done this to her. Tony moved his eyes slowly to the other sofa, where his father lay also drained of life. It looked like he had tried to protect his wife and had been pushed away, as his leg was broken and placed in the wrong direction underneath his body.

Blinking hard, Tony couldn't fight back a bombardment of huge tears, which had started to roll down his face.

"No, No NO! This is not supposed to happen." Tony balled, wiping his hands over his forehead and then slowly down his face.

Excess saliva formed between Tony's lips, similar to a spider's web, as he let out an almighty cry,

"I am supposed to outlive you guys, watch you grow really old and be there for you in your last frail years." Tony's voice distorted with anger and grief, let out a final cry. "Why, why, have you taken them? I've done everything you have asked of me, why couldn't you have spared them?"

With eyes full of tears, he looked around the room now taking in detail other than his parent's bodies. He noticed an impressive looking brochure, which appeared to be for a loft conversion on the coffee table. Tony advanced slowly towards the table and carefully picked the brochure up. Folding it so it fitted in his inside jacket pocket, he used his other hand to take his mobile phone from his jeans pocket. Dialling 999 he made the call to inform the Police.

Chapter Sixteen

Four years later, the UK population was approximately 65,000,000, of which approximately 7 million were vampires. Melinda not looking a day older was having a tough time, separating potential clients who were human and not vampires themselves. She found that if the man resisted paying up front, his agenda normally meant she was on the menu for feeding and impregnating. Her criteria of earning money, feeding and satisfying her high sex drive, meant that she had to really vet her clients before proceeding. She had several near misses with clients who were in fact vampires. She found that turning into her vampire form, usually gave them enough of a fright to avoid any real serious harm.

Recognised that it was no longer safe to go out at night for any reason, supermarkets close their doors at 6pm religiously, petrol stations no longer provide 24 hour opening. Ordering a pizza had become a thing of the past, considered too risky to let a stranger into your home, or risk the delivery person becoming the meal. Public houses had diminished by a shocking 80%, only a few dare open. Virtually impossible to hire a bar person this profession has become a highly paid job, for the ones who were willing to take the risk. On every other streetlight, they were fitted with a 360-degree flood light in an attempt to make the streets feel a little safer. The news no longer smoke screened the truth and charts vampire incident locations in an attempt to provide a service of calculating the high-risk zones.

Women were physically feared more than men, as it was understood that the women kill when they feed, instead of turning their prey. People no longer feared the knife gang culture that used to terrorise the streets.

The census of opinion of people felt like very small fish in a big pond, constantly on guard for that bigger fish trying to eat them. In addition to the population being taken over by vampires, the rate of new born human babies was dramatically falling. People were scared to meet people and make relationships thus procreation was on the decline. The Government recognised that the threat that faced them was one much more serious than terrorism, war with other countries. Even the fear of killer flu, could not spread as quickly as the vampire colony had. The Government deployed specialist attack teams, called VET's (Vampire Eradication Teams) although it was not yet known to them, how to successfully kill a vampire; these boys had every gadget, technology and weapons available to them.

With a similar outbreak confirmed in China all countries were on high alert, banning flights and all other forms of transport from China and the UK, to their shores.

Think Tanks worked around the clock, trying to discover the link between China and the UK and how the infestation started. The opinion was if they could work out how it all started, they might be able to stop it. In the meantime:

Ed a VET soldier controlled the armoured carrier by using two joysticks. The vehicle the size of about a small car moved at the assigned speed limit. About two years ago, the government installed Wi-Fi speed transmitters on to lamp posts, which carried the speed limit sign. These transmitters talked to the vehicles engine management and restrict the hydrogen driven vehicle to whatever the lamp post sign indicates. Although the armoured carrier had a top speed of 60mph it is difficult to control much over 40mph and comfortably plods along at thirty.

Ed concentrated hard on the multiple monitors within the cockpit. The vehicle, an X-A500 built out of the latest armour plated alloy, which structurally could withstand missile and focused laser attacks. In addition to its impregnable skin it also had an iron field surrounding it. For the force field to operate the cabin had to be airtight. With no view holes, Ed totally relied on the sixty onboard micro cameras, to access what surrounds him.

The X-A500 also equipped with the latest thermal imaging, was capable of separating the heat of a flea on a cat through an 8" wall.

Ed felt safe in his Trojan horse, except for the fact he only had twelve hours of oxygen per surveillance shift. Listening to the rumble of the vehicles six wheels bound along the road, he missed the roar of a powerful engine of previous models. The X-A500 was totally powered by hydrogen using the latest cell technology, which provided it with long distance operation but made it almost silent in motion.

Finishing his sweep, he stopped at the end of Camberley's one- way system. Looking at the onboard computer he noticed the time being 20:30hrs and all scanners clear. The X-A500 constantly communicated with the command centre, all data received from the cameras and vitals of the driver were sent per second to the main servers. This occurs for two reasons, mainly if for any reason the X-A500 were to be taken out of action, all data would be saved. This was important as the VET's had ultimate power and if the enemy was believed to be sighted, they had full authorisation to shoot to kill. Ed had yet to activate the weapons systems but deep down wanted to unleash the X-A500's might.

Tilting joystick one forward the X-A500 responded and quickly purred up to 30mph. Ed looked at monitor four and noticed a car behind, with the speed restrictors in place he was not worried about slowing it down. The restrictors did have some benefits.

Then it happened, Ed noticed on monitor six a thermal image of a female being held over a parked car by a larger man. Reacting to his years of military training he entered the personal pin code into the control system touch pad. Activating the weapons system, compressed air could be heard as access panels slid to allow the laser turrets and machine guns to raise and spring in to life. Bobbing with the motion of X-A500 the guns locked onto wherever Ed's pupils looked at on the monitors.

Pressing a button Ed announced his presence over the loud hailer,

"Step away from the woman."

Ed could see the man's eyes light up as he looked at the X-A500.

Taking no notice of Ed's command, the man continued to take the lady from behind.

Now convinced the man was a vampire Ed spoke clearly to the onboard computer,

"Proton laser."

A mapping scope appeared over screen two, which allowed Ed to ensure his shot would be accurate. As the scope locked onto the man's heart, Ed commanded,

"Fire."

A sharp blink of red light filled the gap between the X-A500 and the man. Instantly the powerful beam zapped the man, burning a hole about 3 inches into his chest. Knocked backwards from the force the man fell and landed about two feet from the lady. The second that Ed had activated his weapons the control centre authorised unit cars to the scene. Authorisation from Central Control, allowed the X-A500 engine management to be free and override the speed restrictors. The still air suddenly filled with the sounds of emergency sirens and soon became lit with blue flashing lights.

A unit car opened a channel to the lady,

"Please Miss, run towards us."

Still very much in shock she tried to react but instead remained motionless spread over a car.

The officer understanding her condition leapt from his squad car and ran towards the lady. Taking her hand gently he calmly said,

Man's Natural Predator

"Please you must come with me. Please"

Sobbing uncontrollably she looked at the Police officer vacantly. Without delay Officer Woods picked up the lady and placed her on his shoulders in a fireman's lift.

Walking rapidly back to his squad car, he felt the intense heat of the laser beam on the back of his neck, as another bean struck the vampire one more time. Ed astounded that the vampire had got up from the first six thousand degree beam, commanded the laser to shoot again. Ed thought hitting the vampire twice in short concession may kill it.

Ed watched his monitors closely, whilst the vampire lay still on the ground.

"Control command, this is X-61552. I have engaged the enemy, Sir it won't die. I repeat it won't die." Ed informed his commanding officer, as he watched the vampire rise to his feet again.

"Machine Gun, Fire!"

The machine gun firing 600 rounds per minute, armed with 30mm silver bullets, peeled off 300 rounds into the vampire. House curtains twitched as the sound of the immensely powerful gun, ripped hundreds of bullets threw the air. Knocking the vampire several feet from his standing position, Ed watched his monitors.

Taking no chances Officer Woods and his team started their squad cars and moved out.

Ed stayed in position for several minutes to establish the outcome. Switching between monitors two and three Ed used thermal imaging and clear night vision to watch the vampire.

"Err Euston, we have a serious problem, the silver bullets don't work either. I am going to launch exploding shells."

Watching the vampire get to his feet once again, he waited for the targeting system to confirm target locked, between the vampire eyes.

"Fire!" Ed yelled. A thumping sound bellowed, as a 60mm shell zoomed towards the vampire's head. Sinking deep into the vampire's brain, he again fell to the floor. Three seconds passed, feeling like an hour, Ed watched his monitors intensely. The exploding shell could be heard for approximately two miles but the sound of Ed's cheer could be heard all over the nation. Fragmenting the vampire's head into thousands of bits he finally stayed down.

"Yahoo, they can be killed; you got to take their heads off. Repeat their heads are the hot target."

Ed's transmission broadcasted to all units, shed new light on the war against the creatures of the night.

The morning news on all channels covered no other news, than the top story 'VAMPIRES CAN DIE.' Fuelling human optimism and sending a stiff message to the creatures of the night, that their days were numbered would hopefully bring normality back to the UK. Understanding their weakness, officers armed with exploding bullets enforced the streets the very next day.

When in war, a major advantage is the element of surprise and the enemy not knowing your strategy. The trouble with your enemy being able to watch the TV news the same as everyone else, had a serious adverse effect.

Even the women vampires realised that they could no longer rely on tempting their victims with good old fashion sex techniques. Knowing they were vulnerable it was understood that they needed to become more inventive with their strikes. The Count happy with the size of the UK vampire population, sent telepathic communications to all male vampires to abandon reproduction instincts and advised them clearly that: 'Man will not stop until we are all eradicated, for our survival we must ensure we become the dominant race and lower their numbers to the extent they fear us and they will go into hiding, not us."

With the derivative clearly set, the smart vampires became true hunters taking their prey effortlessly and frequently.

Chapter Seventeen

Wendy fidgeted in an attempt to get comfortable. It had been hot that day and the night was still in the low twenties. Listening to the fan oscillate she pulled her half of the quilt off of her.

"Go to sleep will you?" Jim her husband, grumpily asked.

"Sorry it is so hot in here." She replied.

"I know but I have a big presentation tomorrow, I need to get some sleep."

Turning, she moved over to the far side of the bed. Wendy closed her eyes and tried to go to sleep. Although she had not recalled drifting off, she stirred from her sleep as she subconsciously thought she heard an abnormal sound.

"Did you hear that?" she asked.

Moving over, almost trying to get away from Wendy he grunted and did not answer.

"Jim, I am sure I heard something downstairs." She confirmed in a panic stricken voice.

Now awake Jim raised his head, moving his head in a radar motion to utilise both ears.

"Honey, are you trying to piss me off, I can't hear anything, now go to sleep!"

Slamming his head into the pillow, he pulled the corner up covering his ears. Fifteen seconds had not passed and Jim was again snoring and in a deep sleep.

Wendy not convinced lay, her eyes shut but her senses acutely aware of noises around her. Moving her head slightly from her pillow, she thought she heard a floor board creek. Allowing about thirty seconds to pass, she thought 'I must be going nuts' and closed her eyes tighter to return to sleep.

Cringing with every breath from Jim, as his snoring volume increased, she felt like she would never get back to sleep. She contemplated digging her elbow into him but refrained. After about ten minutes Jim finally stopped snoring, taking a big inhale Wendy thought she could finally get some rest. Feeling her eyes become very heavy she felt herself drifting off. A loud creek startled Wendy, this was definitely a floor board and it sounded as if it was in the room. Sitting bolt upright she grabbed Jims hand and stated,

"You must have heard that!" as she reached for the lamp to turn the light on, the 100w bulb illuminated the room she looked at Jim for a reaction.

Turning white with fear she looked at the Vampire, who's hand she was holding, as his intense eyes locked onto her. Blood still dripping from his fangs, nervously she moved her eyes, without moving her head to look at Jim. He lay there drained of life with two puncture wounds in his neck, the holes swollen almost as if quarterised. Wanting to scream, Wendy did not know what to do next. Like a rabbit trapped in car headlights she froze and waited for his next move. Feeling his grip increase on her hand she knew he was not going to let her go. The glow in his eyes increased as he hissed, exposing his long fangs, she shuddered with fear. Climbing onto the bed he took her hand and forced it up over her head.

"What do you want from me, you've killed my husband please leave me alone." Wendy begged.

Taking her other hand he crossed it over her indicating to her, he wanted her to move onto all fours. Placing his left hand on her throat, he squeezed holding her in position. Lifting her night dress up, he ripped off her knickers exposing her vagina, ready for him to invade her.

Thrusting hard and fast he took her from behind, releasing his grip slightly on her throat, he positioned his head next to hers.

"Do you want to live or die?" he asked in a dark and husky voice.

Wendy was in her late thirties and had always taken good care of her body. Naturally a good looking woman, the Vampire felt she could be of use to the vampire colony. Reaching under her arm he cupped one of her swinging breasts and increased his vigour. Wendy sobbing in fright could not speak, as she felt his member going in and out of her, she could only think of Jim lying dead on the bed next to her whilst she was being raped.

"Die!" she screamed.

"I thought so," the vampire said in a knowing calculated voice.

Sinking his fangs into her neck he drank, whilst he still pumped Wendy from behind. Releasing his sperm he jittered slightly but continued to drink. The pain and shock killed Wendy before she was actually empty of blood.

Releasing his grip from her neck, he let Wendy's limp body fall to the bed. Licking his lips he turned to leave the room.

Although the Police and VET's now knew how to kill the enemy, the war was not going in their favour. With the nightshift coming to an end, all units reported in their achievements for the night. Nationally only nineteen vampires were slaughtered, against the many humans the vampires took, the battle was seriously being lost.

In an effort to balance the success rate, day units prowled the streets providing a 24 hour security. Each vampire slayed would be broadcast all over the news, again outshined by the news of many fresh murders.

Ed rotated his shifts to cover the afternoon to late evening as he had not seen his wife for nearly a straight week. Getting in to his X-A500 the computer clocked his entry at 3pm. Ed sat and re-positioned his side arm to make his seat more comfortable. Ed a giant of a man standing nearly six foot four inches, had to squeeze himself into the small allterrain vehicle. Placing the full harness over each shoulder and clipping it over his waist, he had to adjust the straps from his colleague's smaller frame.

Three hours into his patrol, Ed decided he preferred the night shift and pondered how he would break it to his wife. Looking at monitor four he shook his head in disgust as a car tried to overtake the space aged vehicle. Tempted to press the thruster button, which was designed to allow the vehicle to jump vast gaps in an emergency, he thought better of it. He could not understand why the car was trying to pass him on a single stretch, where speed restrictors applied and his vehicle looked like something out of Mars Mission. He could only assume that because the other driver could not physically see him inside his streamline tank that he could pass. Opening the loud hailer channel, Ed cautioned the driver,

"Please stand down from this dangerous driving behaviour."

Almost instantly the driver repositioned himself behind Ed's vehicle. The A-X500 had a clever algorithm, which constantly listened to external sounds and filtered these sounds from the cockpit, only permitting what it felt to be abnormal to be heard.

The sound of screeching tyres made Ed look at monitor one, where he could clearly see a car come to an abrupt holt. He watched as the passenger door flung open and a woman grabbed a member of the public, pointing a gun at the man she forced him into the back seat. The car sped off, it had obviously had its restrictor disabled, Ed not sure if this was vampire activity knew a crime was taking place so engaged.

Radioing through his status, Ed disabled his restrictor and armed his weapons.

Pushing joystick one forward hard, the X-A500 obediently responded and rapidly reached maximum speed. Ed focussing on all monitors, like a boy playing a computer game, he reacted to the information bombarding him from all screens. Flicking up the manual override for voice command, he pressed the trigger on joystick one momentarily. The chain machine gun mounted on the front of the vehicle, spat out several hundred rounds, ripping the cars suspension and wheels to bits. Watching the back door fly open, Ed could not believe his eyes, as the man hurled from the car bounced and rolled onto the road in front, finally going under the three axles of his vehicle. Watching the driver and the lady passenger leap out of the stopped car he realised that the vampires were working as a team. Trying to feed before the dark set in so to avoid the increased patrol cars.

Locking the driver in his sights he pressed the trigger again, moving his eyes to the lady passenger he unleashed a bombardment of bullets into her. Driving the A-X500 right up to where the two lay motionless, he deactivated the force field and opened the hatch. Leaping over the polished curves of his vehicle he took his side arm which was loaded with exploding 9mm rounds.

Walking up to the driver, he pushed the man onto his back with his foot. Raising his gun he positioned the laser sight between his eyes.

"I want to see your face as I pull the trigger!" Ed muttered

The man vampire stirred as his wounds healed, opening his eyes he looked up at Ed firstly with anger then fear as he noticed the gun pointing at him. Without hesitation Ed pulled the trigger and moved onto the lady passenger.

As he stood over her, the male vampire's head exploded, splattering warm parts of his brain in a 3 meter radius. Wiping a chunk of the male vampire from his face, Ed stood and waited.

The lady vampire's eyes twitched as she began to regain consciousness. Ed unloaded a round into her forehead. Walking away from her and back to his X-A500, he marched with a bound in his step, the sound of her head exploding brought a sick smirk to his face. Climbing back into his vehicle he hummed the melody to 'Another one bites the dust.'

Chapter Eighteen

Tony had graduated from his one year course a black belt and wanted to learn other cultures and arts. Ninjutsu originated from Japan and provided Tony with an excellent base, he had become a formidable student. He wanted a Chinese stance to balance his mindset and skills. He had then booked a three year life school with Sholin Priests in China. Leaving the monks a reformed man, he ventured his way to the airport and modern society. Although he had not gained a certificate to state he was an expert in their form of Kung- fu, the fact he was allowed to leave meant he had passed the tests of life set upon him.

As he sat on the plane, which was destined for Heathrow, he couldn't understand why it was so empty. The Boeing 757 only had a total of six passengers, which he thought could not realistically be a profitable flight. Dismissing this thought, he reassured himself with the thought he was returning to England, so did not really care if the airline was making a loss. The 13hr 20min flight seemed to last forever. Tony was very excited about returning to the UK and had spent the last four years thinking of nothing else.

The landing was a bumpy one, Tony remained calm. His training had taught him not to react but to ascertain and establish the threat. After the plane swerved sideways several times, all wheels of the landing gear connected with the runway with a thud, a text book British Airways landing. As the jumbo came to a standstill, the "fasten seatbelt" light disappeared, acknowledging it was safe to exit the plane.

Tony collected his suitcases from the carousel and moved towards Customs. He had been awarded a samurai type sword, which had to fly separate to his luggage. Tony knew he was going to have a problem getting clearance to bring it into the country and prepared himself for an argument.

Handing over his certificate of ownership to the Customs Officer, Tony took a deep breath in anticipation for a stiff conversation. The Customs Officer looked over the paperwork in great detail. A plump man with a dry skin problem, whose debris, covered his right shoulder of his jumper, paused and then stamped it with Cleared Customs.

Before Tony could even breathe a sigh of relief the man said,

"I don't blame you bringing this with you Sir. With all those vampires out there everyone should have one of these."

Taking the sword, which was safely housed in a long leather sheaf, Tony now understood why the flight was so empty. Tony had tried over the last four years to dismiss the thoughts of his own infection and vampires, as it brought back floods of guilt and memories of his parents. Reaching into his inside jacket pocket he fumbled and pulled out the brochure of the loft conversion company. The brochure faded and tattered; it was of huge importance to Tony and he had kept it with him at all times over the last four years.

Before Tony had set off for China, he had returned his Aston Martin as it was a company asset of Life Savers. He had informed the Bank that he would be out of the Country for several years and not to freeze his account due to there being no activity on it.

Renting a modest car, Tony left the airport and travelled to his luxury home in Surrey.

Several days had passed and Tony had settled back into the house. He only had a few immediate issues to attend to, like purchasing a new fridge. He couldn't believe that he had left a half pint of milk in there before turning it off and leaving. The smell, being stubborn enough to convince Tony it was not going to go away, he decided to throw it and get a new one.

Sitting quietly Tony pondered, although he was watching the TV he was not really taking any of it in. Looking up and around the room he rubbed his face, convincing himself what he was just about to do was the correct time. Unfolding the brochure for the loft conversion company, he reached forward picking up the phone. Not knowing if the person he wished to meet still worked for the company. Not even knowing the man's name or if he were even still alive, Tony made an appointment for a sales rep to visit. Agreeing on a time and date of two days time, Tony trusted his instincts and felt he soon would have closure.

Tony decided he would pop out for a bite to eat and have a pint. He had not been tempted by the forbidden evils of alcohol over the last four years of his intense training regime. Tony now in excellent shape, his body a finely tuned specimen of a man, oozed strength and flexibility but really longed for a cold pint and a chicken burger with fries.

He had not really noticed the massive changes on his trip from the airport to his home as his concentrated on the many new controls of the hire car. Driving to the high street as he knew it, he placed his left indicator on and parked the car. Getting out of the car, he took his time to close the door and tried to take in the baron emptiness of the street. He wouldn't have been surprised if a large chunk of tumble weed came rolling past him, to really set the scene as a ghost town. Arming the alarm of the car, he slowly and cautiously walked down the street. Reaching in his jacket pocket he took out his flight tickets from China. He scanned the detail to obtain the date, 2012 being confirmed by the ticket, he could not believe so much had changed in only four years. Looking down at his watch he checked it was not silly o'clock and he was not all messed up with jetlag. With the correct time confirmed, Tony advanced down the street. Passing unused shop after shop, he finally came to a bar which appeared to be open. Slowly opening the metal gated door that covered the main entrance, Tony took a few seconds to observe the detail of the bar.

Noting three men sitting drinking coffee, one old tramp looking man just sitting and a young lad who could not be much over sixteen sat playing on a hand held games console. Steadily, walking to the bar counter he felt that he was being watched, although all that were in the room did not appear to look up. Waiting patiently to be served Tony took another sweep of the room.

"Hi can I help you?" a strong voice asked.

With no one in sight behind the bar, Tony leant over the counter to find a man crouched on the floor holding a shotgun.

"Hey, what the fuck is going on here? Is it illegal to get a pint nowadays?"

The barman got up from his hiding place and held the gun pointing at Tony's forehead.

"No Sir, it is not illegal, just very dangerous. Slowly come this side of the bar and pour the drink you want. I will be watching you, any funny business and I'll empty all six cases into you."

Tony not totally understanding what he had done, or what was going on slowly moved to the other side of the bar. Making sure not to make any sudden movements he quickly looked on the shelves to find a pint glass. Taking his perfectly poured pint back to the other side of the bar, Tony wisely spoke,

"If I were your enemy, do you think it a wise idea to inform me how much ammunition your gun holds?"

Whilst the barman thought about Tony's question, Tony took a big slug of his pint. Nearly drinking ¾ of the pint, Tony pulled the glass away from his lips and exhaled a large,

"Ahhh, you know I have not had a pint for four years. That tastes like nectar."

Closing his eyes momentarily, as he enjoyed the buzz bouncing off his taste buds, he noticed the barman lowering his gun.

"What, was that the initiation, sink a pint?" Tony asked,

"No, if you were one of them you would not be able to do that without throwing it straight back up."

"One of whom?" Tony inquisitively asked.

Looking very confused, the barman not sure if Tony was joking or not asked,

"You're kidding right?"

"No pal, I've been in Japan then China for the last four years cut off from civilisation."

With this the barman picked his gun back up and aimed it at Tony. Reading the barman's body language, Tony noticed his grip on the trigger increased. Looking down the barrel directly into the barman's eyes, Tony calculated he would soon be pulling the trigger. Not wishing to take a blast and then get up unhurt, Tony needed to act quickly.

Dropping his pint glass, he waited for the glass to impact with the floor before jumping towards the barman as well as upwards. Grabbing a supporting metal bar, Tony swung from the bar, performing a double flip to land behind the barman. Knocking the rifle upwards, as he swiped the man's feet from underneath him, Tony pointed the gun at the him. In a calm and positive voice Tony said,

"If I wanted to kill you, I would have for making me pour my own pint."

Lifting the gun to indicate he was not going to shoot the barman, Tony extended his hand to help him back to his feet. Chucking the rifle horizontal, making the barman catch it with both hands, Tony walked back to the other side of the bar.

"Another pint please I seem to have accidently dropped the last one."

Feeling safe for the first time in a long time, the barman quickly poured Tony a beer.

"On the house, sorry mate for the misunderstanding you gotta appreciate, I have to be careful."

Tony now convinced of the problem he referred to, said,

"Do you mean vampires?"

"Yes, they are taking China by storm so I just put two and two together and got six."

Tony had developed an excellent peripheral sense and heard a man about twelve stone creep in the door. Still talking to the barman, he turned his head to take a look at the new arrival. Smirking slightly, Tony noticed a glow surrounding the man and turned his attention back to the barman.

"Hey fella, you know the rules, pour yourself a drink before you go mingling with my locals." the barman ordered,

The vampire looked at the barman, who was now pointing his shotgun at him. The vampire knowing he would fail the test quickly considered his options. Thinking he could easily feed off of the young lad and use him as a human bullet shield he nervously edged his way closer to the lad.

"Hey you, walk this way or I will open fire."

Whilst they entered into deadlock, neither of them had noticed Tony leave the bar area and silently move close to the lad. Making his move, the vampire lunged forward, fangs bared, his face turned to a crinkly demon form. Turning his head to engage with the lad's neck, he found himself changing direction. Tony performing a spinning side kick, knocked the vampire backwards, impacting into a white Roman looking pillar.

Standing in a stance which indicated he was obviously an expert in some martial art, Tony looked at the vampire and waited as the vampire rebuilt his ribs from Tony's kick.

With glowing eyes, the vampire looked at Tony and hissed,

"I'm going to enjoy watching you twitch as I suck the last drop of blood out of you."

Tony moved a step closer to the vampire and boldly said,

"I will make it quick for you."

Not fazed by Tony's statement, the vampire aggressively advanced to try and eat Tony. As he did, Tony entered into an elaborate cartwheel gymnastic manoeuvre, spinning his entire body 360 degrees and rotating in full three times, he passed the vampire.

Stopping and looking behind him, he casually walked back towards the bar. Releasing a metal handle from his left hand, it sprang back into his right hand. The barman, who had froze and not even tried to take a shot, watched a strong lightweight wire retract into Tony's hand, as if he were retracting a tape measure.

Looking at the vampire, he noticed his head was one side of the room and his body the other.

Taking a fifty pound note from his money clip, Tony casually chucked it on the bar whilst saying,

"Sorry about the mess, they have a habit of spurting all over the place."

Without any further words, Tony walked out of the bar.

Amazed with what had just happened the barman uttered,

"Who is that guy?"

Chapter Nineteen

Tony waited patiently for the rep of the loft conversion company to arrive. Although highly trained and immortal, Tony felt nervous about meeting this man. Looking at his watch again, another whole 30 seconds had past. Standing to look out of the window, he noticed a car pull up outside the gates. Tony calmly moved towards the intercom positioned in the kitchen to buzz the rep in.

"Hello, it's Mr Richards from Loft to Rooms."

Pressing the release button, Tony allowed the car to enter his driveway. Watching on the CCTV, Tony tracked the red Vauxhall Astra Sport as it slowly and carefully drove up the driveway.

Keen to get a clear image of the man, Tony continued to watch the CCTV monitor intensively. Watching a young man in his mid twenties athletically get out of the car, Tony felt that this was his man. Tony had trained religiously and conditioned himself over the last four years for this moment. He felt that even if this guy doesn't glow he would still beat him up.

Waiting for the door bell, Tony made his way to the front door. Taking the brochure out of his back pocket, Tony looked at it briefly one last time before the clear and precise Ding Dong sounded.

Returning the brochure to his back pocket, Tony opened the door.

"Hi I am James Richards of Loft to Rooms. I have an appointment with Tony."

Before he finished his introductions, Tony interrupted and said,

"Hi that's me, please come in."

Tony had spent many hours being taught to control emotions but struggled to hold back a large smirk as the rep glowed.

Showing James through to the lounge, Tony thought, 'When shall I slay him?' He had thought many times over and over in his mind of taking this man down. Now with the man stood in front of him, he failed to actually have a plan.

Allowing James to sit and get prepared to deliver the pitch of the century, Tony asked,

"Have you done any conversions locally, maybe someone I could speak to about your work?"

Still pulling various brochures from his brief case, James replied,

"Yes many, I will of course get a list for you to contact when I return to the office." Releasing his bottom button of his suit jacket, James widened his legs ready for his pitch.

"If I could ask firstly what is your aspiration for the space of the current loft?"

Tony not really interested in converting his loft, moved to the coffee table and picked up his glass of red wine.

"Would you like a glass?" Tony teased

"No Sir not whilst working but thank you."

Tony remaining silent swirled the red wine round in his large bulbous glass. James mesmerised by the blood looking fluid, could think of nothing else but wrapping up this boring meeting and feeding. Snapped out of his trance and asked,

"Sir, your intentions for the loft space please?"

"So do you feed on the second appointment then? When you collect the deposit cheque I guess, you probably still get your commission that way?"

Feeling very uncomfortable James rose to his feet, replacing the important brochures and documents back into his brief case. He nervously looked up at Tony and said,

"I thought from the moment I saw you, this would be a waste of time and I hate tyre kickers."

As James placed the last document into his brief case, Tony tossed the four year old faded brochure onto the coffee table, inches from James's hand. Recognising the old design of artwork on the brochure, James understood that they had not used this design for over three years. Looking up slowly at Tony, his eye twitched, he was trying to control not changing as he felt vulnerable.

"What's going on here pal? Do you get your kicks out of wasting sales people's time?"

Tony leapt over the coffee table with stealth like precision, as he passed over it he took the brochure from James hand. With his other hand he placed it tightly around James's neck. Holding the brochure just millimetres from James's face, Tony asked,

"Do you know who the last person was to hold this brochure, Do you?"

Shaking his head rapidly from side to side James indicated he did not. Although being a vampire usually scares people enough to overpower them, James could tell by the look in Tony's eyes he was not going to be intimidated.

"Let me tell you, you piece of lifeless shit. I can feel that the last person to hold this brochure was my father. He dropped it when he tried to save my mother from your bite. Does Mr Sherman ring any bells? Now listen, I understand everything about your kind. It is actually my fault you buggers have taken over the country. I am going to make this as slow as I can."

Squeezing harder on James's windpipe, Tony provoked him to turn. Watching James's eyeballs roll in their sockets and his eyelids flicker, with no reaction from James, he suddenly doubted himself if he was in fact the right man.

Releasing his grip as he threw James on to the sofa, his doubts vanished. The glow of James had intensified and he turned into his demon form. Throwing his head towards Tony rapidly whilst letting off a cougar type growl, James now meant business.

"Yes I remember now, your father begged me to stop after I had tossed him off of me. I took extra pleasure in devouring him. I remember looking into his eyes as I tore his throat out." James growled.

Tony stood tall and strong, detaching his emotions, his stare became intense, indicating to James that he had pressed a button, which he should have maybe left alone. Reaching into the inside of Tony's jacket, he took out a throwing star which he had adapted to suit its new purpose. With an accurate flick of his wrist, the bladed star flew through the air cutting a large segment from James's neck. Watching James fall to his knees, Tony moved closer and deployed a front kick to James's forehead.

Sending his head backwards and nearly breaking his head clean off, James somersaulted backwards. Holding his neck he tried to stem the violent flow of blood spurting from his wound. Releasing one hand, he placed it on the floor and tried to get back to his feet. The spinning oscillating sound of another star zooming towards him made him look up at where he believed Tony to be standing. It was too late to do anything as the star cut through his wrist, severing his hand. Falling back to the floor, Tony said,

"Stay down. I am going to let you know how it feels for every little last drop of blood to leave your body, before I take your head off."

The sound of another star hurtling its way towards James took priority over what Tony had just said. He looked up like an animal caught in a bear trap and awaited the blade to strike. A thud, as the star terminated its journey into the wall meant it had taken its target. James looked down on the polished wooden floor at his other hand cut from his wrist. Forced to kneel upright with his stumps crossed in front of his chest he could not balance any other way. He turned his attention to

Tony as he felt his body becoming faint and heavy. With so much damage to his nervous system and body his vampire DNA couldn't repair any tissue in time.

Tony only inches away from James, removed his jacket and reached over his left shoulder. Removing the deadly sharp samurai sword from its sheath, James knew this would soon be over. Leaning slightly forward to provide a clean shot at the back of his neck, James awaited his fate. With one almighty blow James was free from his nightmare and could finally rest in peace. The sound of his head bopping on the solid wooden floor confirmed James was free.

Holding the sword tightly in one hand, Tony observed the decapitated body. A sense of fulfilment rushed over Tony's body, as he thought of the burning last images of his parents. Placing the sword back into its sheath, Tony cleared his mind and prepared to clean up. Picking the head up by its hair and dragging the body he made his way to the car.

Arriving back at the house about an hour later, Tony knew he had to clean the blood soaked lounge. Not enthusiastic about this task he decided to bypass the lounge and head for the fridge. The beer he had put in it when he first got it would certainly be cold by now.

Turning on the LCD in the kitchen Tony flicked on the news. He needed to catch up on the Count's developments and understand the magnitude of the growth, whilst he was away. As the screen and the volume adjusted, Tony started to watch the gardening programme, as he took another sip from his beer can. Thinking he must get a glass, when his priorities seriously altered. The gardening show stopped in mid flow and was interrupted for an important news flash. The pretty news presenter immaculately groomed and professional in her delivery looked sternly at the camera and paused momentarily. Her face looked concerned as if this news actually affected her personally. Taking a deep breathe she alerted the nation of its new potential fate.

"The President of the United States has warned both the United Kingdom & China that if they do not convince the U.S that the infection outbreak is being controlled in an acceptable level, they will intervene. The President has assured both countries that if the outbreaks are not contained and eradicated within one month, they will have no reservations of wiping us off the face of the planet and I quote Protect Man Kind.'

The U.S. has indicated that they will take action with Nuclear Strikes, if they are not convinced the threat is being dealt with in an effective manner."

The presenter then added on how the government plans to provide the U.S. with the reassurance they seek.

Tony shell shocked by this condemning news looked at the screen vacantly. Leaning forward he rested his elbows on the kitchen island and held his head in his hands. Rubbing his face as if he had just woken up he thought

'Why did I open that coffin, if I had just left it alone none of this would have happened. Chosen one, my arse, fool more like it.'

Just when he thought it could not get any worse, the presenter closed her broadcast with,

"Do you know this man?"

The camera panned to an artist's impression of a man who looked very much similar to Tony.

"Officials are pleading for anyone who knows this man to come forward, however insignificant you feel the lead may be. This man has allegedly single handily beheaded a vampire, without even breaking a sweat. Officials are keen to speak with this man and wish to work with him closely to defeat the vampire race."

Tony listened to the presenter further but the words became mumbles as he drifted into his own thoughts. He did not wish for this attention nor did he wish to become an innocent fugitive who could no longer show his face in public. He certainly could not collaborate with the government, as if they were to find he was not one hundred percent human, they would certainly treat him as the enemy. The thought of waiting for a nuclear attack to disintegrate him gave him a brief feeling of hope to end his immortality. Unsure of his intentions Tony decided to seek guidance from another can of lager.

The Count also observed the news intently in China and absorbed the might of the U.S. threat. He had not anticipated a strike from another country and stood still momentarily to ponder. Looking out into the busy streets still bursting with fresh food bustling pass him, he took his wallet from his back pocket, checking he had all of his bank cards. Placing his wallet back into his pocket, he turned slowly 360 degrees and vanished into thin air.

Materialising in a spot approximately one hundred yards from the Empire State Building, the Count looked around him as the thin mist cleared, taking in the views of his new home.

Chapter Twenty

One eye flickered as Tony scratched the other eye that was winning the race of waking up. Taking a deep breath expanding his chest to maximum, he stretched preparing his body for the day ahead of him. A slight cracking sound broke his stretch, as he realised he was laying on the TV remote. Sitting up he repositioned his pillows to support his back and took a moment to wake and look around his room. Looking at the remote he thought about turning the TV on but instead slung it to the bottom of the bed. Taking both hands he gently massaged his face either side of his nose, rubbing his hands over his eyes. Slowly shaking his head he shook out the cloudy feeling of the beer he had consumed the night before. It was a long time since he had the pleasure of his tipple and found it hard to leave it at one can.

Tony surprisingly slept well, although the disturbing news had played on his mind prior to drifting off. His thoughts turned to the Count.

'He must know what is going on, he must know that I have not checked on Melinda over the last four years.'

Almost certain he felt that the Count would be paying him a visit today. The feeling he could only imagine to be similar to waiting for a visit from a debt collector. The feeling for someone who cannot pay the debt back, knowing any day now the big muscle man would be breaking the door down with no sympathy of circumstances.

Tony thought, if the count did materialise,

'Should I try and take him on and slay him, or would it be easier to let him slay me. I have not seen his full power yet, I am sure.'

Getting out of bed he made his way to the en-suite to freshen up. Wearing just his y-fronts he stumbled in the correct direction. Even though Tony's body and mind were now perfectly tuned instruments he still found the first thirty minutes after waking up a difficult time.

The invigorating jet of water from his shower injected new life into Tony. Rubbing shower gel over his chiselled abdominals he placed his face directly into the shower jets. Tony thought,

'If I keep drinking to much beer, my six pack will turn into a Lurpak.'

Now fully refreshed and focused, Tony turned his attention to the matters in hand.

'Well one thing I better at least do, is see if Melinda is ok.'

Wearing a T-shirt and jeans, Tony felt he would visit Melinda casually dressed. He did not even know if she was still alive or if she was still living at the same address.

Picking up his overcoat, which had a few surprises tucked away in it, he made for the door. Still confident he would be getting a visit from the Count, he opened the front door cautiously, taking his time to check the path between him and the car to be clear.

Walking confidently towards his car, he monitored his surroundings, similar to a bodyguard checking for enemy threat.

Pressing the remote unlocking his rental and opening the car door, Tony took a brief second to feel the presence of birds tweeting and the leaves rustling in the wind, before getting into the car. Maybe now was not the time, but Tony knew he would at some stage confront the Count.

The drive to London Vauxhall area took about an hour and a half. The streets now quite deserted, Tony parked easily and took in the view of the once bustling region. Switching off the engine and getting out of the car, Tony put on his overcoat as the air had quite a chill to it although the constant talk of Global Warming did not seem to be occurring. Taking a quick sweep of his surroundings, Tony locked the car and walked in the direction of Melinda's flat.

On the path opposite, Tony noticed a young attractive couple walking hand in hand. Admiring this object of beauty, Tony chuckled and thought,

'It's nice to see people still getting on with their lives you can't get in the way of love.'

Taking another three strides, Tony noticed a couple of large men, who had a dim glow surrounding them, closely in tow of the couple.

"You've got to be kidding me, in broad daylight?" Tony muttered.

Looking at the couple, who must be no more than twenty years of age he noticed that they had no idea of what was behind them. Stopping, Tony changed direction taking a large step to cross the road, he quickly retracted his foot and stood patiently on the kerb. A car restricted to thirty passed him, without noticing Tony had nearly walked in its path.

"Fuck it" Tony ranted, as he lost visual of the couple and their predators, who had all turned off the main street.

Checking the road to be clear, Tony walked across in the direction of where he had last seen them. His pace accelerated but not fast enough to break into a jog, Tony feared the worst.

Turning the corner into the side street, he clearly saw the predators had decreased the distance between them and the couple.

Tony not sure if to shout to warn the couple or to observe them, increased his pace to a brisk jog. He decided to travel on the opposite side of the road to the couple, just in case the predator's intentions were not to feed on the them.

Not convinced, Tony increased his gain on them until he reached a safe distance to which he would not be noticed but could intervene if required.

The couple who could obviously feel the predators presence, moved over slightly on the path to allow them to pass. The two love birds oblivious to the potential danger continued with their conversation and romantic stroll. The young lady dressed smartly, wearing a cream coat, tightly pulled into her waste by a belt. The length of her coat revealed a smidgen of her figure hugging skirt. Her knee high boots, occasionally showing their length as she walked added to her classy sexy look. Looking at her boyfriend with misty eyes and intensely listening to his conversation, she did not notice the two large men pass them.

Tony watched to see what the predator's next move was going to be. To his surprise the predator's simultaneously turned and stopped the couple in their tracks. One of the predators pulled a gun from his pocket and assertively pointed it at the young man.

"Right this is what is going to happen. We are going to have some fun with your girlie and then we are going to have you for dinner" The man with the gun informed.

The other man moved in towards the young lad and grasped his neck pinning him to a shop window behind him.

Before the young man could even think about defending his loved one, she seized the opportunity and ran for her life.

"Sorry" she exhaled, as she ran into the distance.

The man with the gun altered his aim, from the defenceless lad to the escapee. With a swift squeeze of the trigger the gun unleashed a mighty blow. Sending a 9mm bullet hurtling towards the young lady, it impacted in her right heel. A dull thud sounded, as the bullet penetrated her leather boot and heel. This sound was quickly silenced by her scream as she fell to the ground in agony.

"I hate runners." The man with the gun said, as he started walking towards the crippled lady.

"Yes, but it does make it better fun, good shot. Now watch your Mrs get spanked by us, for running off like that." The other man added, whilst increasing his grip on the young lad.

With his gun at his side the man slowly walked over to the petrified lady, she tried to get to her feet but the pain proved too much. Looking over her shoulder she started to crawl away from the man as fast as she could. Gritting her teeth in an attempt to numb the pain, she embedded her nails into the pavement as she pulled herself along.

Smiling as the man with the gun approached, he shouted to her,

"I'm going to enjoy sticking my cock in you, then when I am done my friend over there is going to do you as well. As you are so pretty we might both do you at the same time."

Hearing what the man said, the young lad started to thrash in an attempt to break free.

"No you leave her alone you evil bastard!" shouting as loud as he could.

The man holding the young lad in place turned into his vampire form, indicating to the lad his time was up.

Squinting in fear the lad awaited his fate, breaking into fits of tears he muttered,

"Sorry Louise."

To his surprise, as he awaited the feeling of fangs bursting into his neck, a strong bold voice spoke.

"Is this man bothering you?"

The young lad opened his eyes, to see Tony standing close behind the vampire whose fangs were inches off his neck.

Looking over the vampires shoulder, he nervously nodded and blurted,

"Yes Sir, yes he is, help me!"

The vampire turned in astonishment to take a look at the idiot who dare disturb his feed.

Keeping a tight grip on the young lad, the vampire turned his body and stood tall to confront Tony.

"What the hell is wrong with you? Can you not see I am busy?" the vampire asked.

Without answering the vampire, Tony shouted to the other vampire.

"Hey ugly fuck, your mate needs your help over here."

Stopping just in touching distance to the lady, he turned and aimed his gun at Tony. Without hesitation he peeled off four rounds at Tony.

Almost in slow motion Tony watched the bullets accelerate towards him. Taking evasive manoeuvres, Tony managed to dodge two of the bullets. The remaining two slammed into his chest, temporary knocking him off balance. Tony let out a smothered cry before calmly looking down at his body. Wiping over one of the bullet holes, Tony looked at his palm to see how much blood was evident.

"Damn this is one of my favourite shirts, you are really going to wish you had not done that." Tony preached, as he flicked out his right arm across the vampire nearest to him.

The young lad's face changed from one of sheer fright to one of amazement, as Tony stood strong undeterred by the bullets. Then his face turned to a puzzled expression as he felt the vampire's grip slowly loosen from around his neck.

Tony walked towards the other vampire who had now taken a grip of the lady. Tony walked casually towards the vampire. The young lad caught a glimpse of a shiny object running up Tony's right forearm. Focusing harder he could clearly make out that Tony was holding a nine inch knife in reverse grip, with the blade facing outwards up his arm.

Noticing that the vampire, who was just about to eat him, had become very lifeless, he gave the vampire a little push.

"Holly fuck." he gasped, as the vampire fell to the ground like a sack of spuds.

Holding his hand over his mouth, to contain bringing up his breakfast, the lad watched the vampire's head fall in a different direction. Bouncing like a football, the head bounced twice before settling from the paths edge.

"Step away from the lady." Tony ordered as he advanced towards the remaining vampire. Surprised that Tony was still standing the vampire took aim once more and emptied the magazine of his pistol.

Watching the explosion leave the barrel of the gun and a bullet soon after, Tony observed the oncoming bullets, as if in slow motion. Adopting a stealth like panther stance, Tony performed an elaborate gymnastic choreography of spins, front flips and forward rolls, to avoid the onslaught of rounds zooming towards him.

Taking the occasional hit, Tony advanced aggressively towards the vampire and soon stood poised around six foot in front of the worried predator. The vampire stood with a wide stance and pressed the trigger one final time, to hear a piercing click, indicated that the gun was now empty. The vampire looked at it and shook it hard, as if magically it would suddenly be reloaded with a full magazine.

"Give it up and I'll let you live." Tony offered as he stood in a cat like stance.
Coiled like a spring ready to pounce at any given second. Turning his head slightly to eliminate a gust of wind from his hearing, Tony focused his senses on the signals the vampire emitted.
Panicking the Vampire grabbed Louise by her hair and pulled her to her feet. Pointing the gun to her temple he threatened Tony.
"Come any closer and I swear I will plug her."
Louise looked over at her boyfriend Steve, with an expression of desperation. She struggled to see him clearly through her tears, the pain of her gaping wound to her heel seemed to be a little fainter.
Tony looked hard into the vampire's eyes, which were now of their wolf like form. He concentrated hard to ensure his gut instinct that the vampire was bluffing to be correct. Without a millisecond passing, Tony thrust his right arm from his hip in the direction of the vampire. Deploying an extending throwing star which grew from a three inch diameter to a six inch lethal circular blade. The chaos of the mixed emotions became still, watching the star gracefully and angelically cut through the air.

Although appearing to travel in slow motion, the star advanced towards its target with deadly accuracy and at an immense rate. Making an oscillating sound, similar to a helicopter blades, the star struck its target. The pitch of the spinning star altered briefly, as it surgically cut threw its target to again return to its former note, as it made its journey back to Tony.

Catching the obedient star and returning it to its sheath, Tony casually walked towards Louise.

Tony stretched out to support Louise as her weight transferred to her injured foot. The vampire that was providing support to her fell to his knees. Balancing for several seconds on his knees the vampire wobbled, before falling fully forward. The Vampire's head taking a different path rolled down his back, bouncing off the middle of his back and landing hard on to the ground below.

Trying not to scream, Louise held her hands over her mouth, making it harder for Tony to support her.

"It's over now. You need to get to a hospital fast you have lost a lot of blood. Do you or your boyfriend have a phone?"

Not wishing to remove her hands, Louise nodded instead of answering.

Holding her close to his chest, Tony turned his head to look over his shoulder. Jerking his head in a welcoming manner, Tony indicated to Steve to leave the shop window and come over and comfort Louise.

Steve picked up momentum and zoomed towards Tony and his beloved.

"What's your name buddy?"

"Steve, who are you? You must have been shot at least ten times."

"Bullet proof vest, Steve. Now call 999 and get an ambulance here quick. I will wait with you until it gets here, just in case you have any more bother. With her pissing blood all over the place, other vampires will get wind of you!"

"Thanks." Steve replied and looked at Tony in disbelief.

He could clearly see that Tony's T-shirt had bullet holes in it and Tony's skin beaming through each hole. Tony was clearly not wearing a bullet proof jacket.

Once Steve had finished his call, Tony moved side wards to let Steve nestle in under Louise's armpit.

"I thought I had lost you." Steve spoke in a teary voice.

"Hold me, I am starting to feel quite cold." Louise replied.

The sound of the ambulances siren nearing provided a reassuring boost to both Louise and Steve. Tony waited for the ambulance to arrive, screeching to an abrupt holt the emergency crew spilled out. Taking a look at the staff, Tony checked none of them had a certain glow before making his exit. Blending into the background Tony had almost drifted out of sight when Steve turned and shouted.

"Hey man, thanks a million. How can I ever repay you?"

Tony thought for a second and answered,

"When the cops ask you to describe me, say you could not make me out. It all happened too fast."

"You got it, whatever you say and once again thanks man." Steve's face stern and sincere provided Tony with the reassurance Steve was a man of his word.

Chapter Twenty One

Knocking hard on Melinda's door, Tony pondered if firstly she still lived there and secondly if he should in fact slay her.

The thirty seconds Melinda took to get to the door seemed to last for an eternity. Tony looked around the hallway as he waited and turned to walk away when he heard a safety latch being opened.

Returning back to position himself in front of the door, he squinted to try and look through the inspection spy hole.

"Melinda are you in there? It's Tony."

On receipt of hearing his voice the sound of several security latches being released confirmed to Tony that Melinda still lived there.

Cautiously opening the door, Melinda peeped round the edge and looked hard at Tony. Satisfied it was him, she swung open the door and jumped onto him wrapping her legs around his waist.

"Tony it is you, I thought I might never see you again." she said, nestling her head into his neck.

Not concerned she might decide to eat him, Tony enjoyed the moment.

"May I come in?"

"Sorry, I am just so pleased to see you. Come on in, I have so much to talk to you about."

Walking with a boyish bounce in his step, Tony took the opportunity to look Melinda up and down. Still in great shape and if possible more beautiful then before, Tony temporarily dismissed his thoughts of cutting her head off.

"Where have you been all this time?" Melinda asked, whilst pointing the TV remote at her Hi-fi to turn the volume down.

Leaning over to place the remote back on the coffee table, Tony found he was again checking her contours out.

"Hmm, sorry I have been in China!"

"China you say, that would explain the vampire population getting out of control over there."

"No, I had nothing to do with that, Vamps has done that all on his own."

Melinda looked at Tony in an inviting manner and tapped the sofa seat next to her, instructing Tony to join her.

"Who is Vamps?" Melinda asked

"Sorry, you know him as Roberto. I was there on a personal basis, purely coincidental trust me. I knew nothing about their problems, until I recently returned to the UK."

Melinda looked intensively at Tony as he spoke thinking he had really bulked up well and found herself quite attracted to him.

Tony with his newly heightened senses felt a strong chemistry coming from Melinda and scratched his neck in a nervous fidget. He had not been in any form of a relationship with a woman, for the last four years and suddenly found himself quite uncomfortable looking Melinda in the eyes. Changing the subject,

"How have you been? Roberto asked for me to watch over you. He expressed he was very fond of you. You two had something special didn't you?"

A little bit embarrassed by this Melinda dipped her head and looked at Tony almost through her neatly groomed eyebrows.

"It was strange you know. When I think about it, he was quite awful to me really. He only appeared when he wanted his wicked way with me. He was always polite to me whilst impregnating me though. He could have simply killed me I suppose! It was just whilst he was about I felt very drawn to him, I even thought at one point I loved him. Ha, how crazy is that!"

Tony politely smiled and thought,

'Boy she can talk. This would normally bother me, I would normally drift off into Tonysville. Wow, she is so hot. Shame she is a predator of mans blood, otherwise I could quite see myself making a pass at her.'

"Tony am I boring you?"

"No, no, no, I was just thinking what beautiful lips you have, quite mesmerising." Tony rapidly replied, realising he had in fact drifted off to Tonysville and,

'Why did I just say that?'

Tony thought that it was all going horribly wrong, when Melinda broke his erratic panic.

"That is really sweet, thank you. Do you know I have not had a real compliment for many years, well not from someone not paying to do stuff to me, well you know what I mean."

"Sorry where are my manners, do you want a drink or something?" Melinda asked, knowing she did not have a thing in the flat.

Tony took a deep breath and stood from his seat.

"Would it be ok to find a cafe, bar or something? I am quite hungry and I don't suppose you have a lasagne or any other substance for me to eat."

Melinda strangely drawn to his familiarity nodded.

"You mind if I just observe?" she asked whilst, looking in her handbag checking all her make up was present.

Not responding to this, Tony offered his arm in a gentlemanly manner, making Melinda feel quite special.

Arms entwined they left the flat and headed for a cafe, which Melinda knew was still open for business.

Walking the short distance to the cafe almost like a couple in love, Melinda could not believe it. Even before her existence as a predator, her profession made it very difficult to lead any form of romantic activities. Quite bamboozled by this simple gesture she looked up at Tony and thought,

'He is quite handsome, you know. If only I was normal!'

Reaching the bar, Tony looked at it's run down appearance and noted the name 'The Queens Head.' Briefly reminding him of the recent decapitations, he focused his feelings towards Melinda.

Always the gent, Tony opened the door,

"Ladies first."

Not really thinking what might be the other side of the door to greet her, he watched her lift her step delicately over the threshold of the bar entrance. Distracted by her long calves fluting down to her four inch high heels, he thought,

'Man, she is going to get me in trouble or something, focus damn it focus.'

Entering the bar, Melinda held her hand behind her, seeking security from Tony. Stopping just steps inside the doorway she froze and gently tugged on Tony's hand.

Looking over her shoulder Tony looked at the barman aiming a twelve bore shotgun at Melinda.

Quickly thinking, Tony spoke assertively but calmly,

"Hey man, give me a beer and I will prove we are not one of them."

The barman obviously familiar with this drill felt at ease and lowered his aim. Melinda stood still, quite scared of being found out, Tony returned the gentle tug to encourage her to move.

Taking a large sip of his pint, Tony quickly intercepted the barman's next question,

"Is it ok to sit over on that table, I am starving are you still serving food?"

Relieved that he actually had normal clients the barman replied,

"Yes, the menu is on the table. Sorry about pointing a gun in your face Madam. I have to be careful I'm sure you understand."

"Yes of course, don't be silly." Melinda replied. The feeling of being treated like a lady made her feel human again and filled her with a strange feeling of hope.

Sitting at the table they conducted as if a normal couple, Tony made his excuses for Melinda not eating or drinking. Tony's brontosaurus burger, stacked high with three half pounder burgers, separated by bacon, cheese, tomatoes and drenched with every conceivable relish, filled the empty bar with a pleasant meaty smell. Tony looked at Melinda and asked,

"You sure you don't want to join me? Boy I have waited a long time for this sucker."

"Err, gross. Even if I could eat that it would make me heave."

Tony poked his tongue to the edge of his lips to stem the flow of salivation whilst he handled the monstrosity of a burger. Taking a deep bite, Tony looked up at Melinda, who cringed and drew her head back slightly, in disgust as Tony ripped into the burger.

With his mouth still rammed with food, Tony muffled,

"Sorry, but this is gorgeous. No real first date for you is it?" Realising what he had just said, his eyes widened almost double in size. He looked as if he were holding his breath, his mouth tightly shut still occupied with masticated food.

To Tony's surprise, Melinda leant forward slanted her head slightly and smiled. Rubbing his inner calf gently with her foot, which she had just removed from her stiletto, she advanced up his leg.

Placing his shark attacked burger back on its plate. Tony wiped his mouth with a serviette and reached forward to clasp her hand.

"I really feel for you Melinda, I do. I think you are fucking fab, but it's too complicated."

"I know, it is crazy, but I would really like to try!"

The barman noticing their intimate moment smiled and turned up a TV near to the bar, so not to overhear their conversation.

"Hey don't get me wrong, I am nuts about you. I have been since the first time I met you. There is more to this than meets the eye, I don't want to hurt you. You deserve better than that."

Slightly baffled by Tony's cryptic answer, Melinda's attention drifted from Tony's sorrowful eyes to the TV. The news reporter, covering Tony's previous handy work asked,

"Do you know this man? He is being nicknamed & hailed as the 'Exterminator'

witnesses of today's incidents confirm the Surrey slaying to be the same man."

As the camera shot panned to an artist impression of a man looking very similar to Tony, Tony squeezed Melinda's hand.

Slowly turning her head from the direction of the TV back to Tony, Melinda's eyes dragged behind like a child not wishing to go where instructed.

Slowly pulling her hands from Tony's grasp, Melinda asked,

"Do I need to fear you, have you come to slay me?"

Her face hurt, with the thought she had trusted Tony and reached out to him.

"As I said it is complicated, Melinda. No I have not come to slay you. That's the last thing on my mind. With the others, I see them as vermin, predators of human flesh. When I look at you I see a beautiful, elegant lady, sexy of course but I know you are still a good person. In a strange way I also want to see if we could work!"

Sold by Tony's believable speech, Melinda replaced her hands over Tony's and leant forward towards him. Understanding she wished to cement their trust with a kiss, he leant forward and met her half way.

Millimetres away from each others lips, both Tony and Melinda puckered so their lips erratically touched. Sparks of electricity seemed to jump between their lips before they made full contact. Engaging in a passionate kiss, lasting for about three minutes, Melinda pulled away slowly. Her body teeming with sensual pulses, she paused to savour this forgotten feeling.

Taking a seductive breath in over her lips, she slowly opened her eyes,

"Fancy coming back to my place?" focusing her bright blue wide eyes on Tony.

"I thought you would never ask!"

Chapter Twenty Two

Returning to Melinda's flat, Tony felt both excited and nervous about spending some 'quality time' with Melinda. Shutting the door to her flat, she turned to him. She looked up at him with an expression of an innocent virgin, keen to explore new boundaries. Although Tony certainly knew this not to be the case, he couldn't help feeling drawn to her perfection and womanly curves, his eyes locked with her seductive stare.

His natural desire to fornicate with her overwhelmed him, he moved a little closer and held her hands by her finger tips and interlocked his fingers with hers. Pulling her smoothly in close to him, he placed a moist and passionate kiss on her lips. As their kiss intensity increased, Melinda slid her fingers away from his, slowly gliding over his skin, maintaining soft contact with his fingertips until their hands separated. Moving them to his bottom, her hands adventured over the contours of his firm, rock hard buttocks. Placing one hand on each buttock of Melinda's, Tony returned the gesture and manly pulled her in tightly towards his groin area.

Breaking away from their kiss Melinda held her head back and opened her mouth in ecstasy. Admiring the fine lines of her neck, Tony placed soft short kisses along the front of her neck. Starting at the top, slowly moving south towards her chest, Tony thought,

'Oh my god, she is fucking horney. She smells like priceless perfume and tastes so clean and fertile. I better not cum in my pants, Grandma on the bog, Grandma on the bog!'

Placing one hand on the side of Tony's head, Melinda arched her fingers pressing her finely shaped fingernails into his scalp guiding his kisses with pin point accuracy to areas of sensitivity on her skin. Releasing his grasp of her behind, he delicately gripped either side of her silk blouse. Pulling his hands apart with just enough force, her buttons popped off her blouse revealing her plump firm breasts. Tinkering on the laminate flooring the buttons settled. Only to be disturbed by Tony's shoes, as he moved his feet to lower his body to comfortably maintain his head at Melinda's chest height.

Leaving her breasts in her bra, Tony gently kissed her cleavage and tongued her nipples through the delicate material of the bra.

Lowering her head and pulling his into her breasts, Melinda enjoyed Tony treating them as sensitive, sensual items and not kneading them as if making bread.

Widening her stance and using the door to lean back on, Melinda wrapped one leg around one of his strong legs and caressed it up and down his firm hamstring.

Pulling his head away from Melinda, Tony sincerely looked into her eyes and said,

"Not here, I want this to be special."

As a professional, Melinda had become used to being treated as a sex object and not a person with feelings.

Before Melinda could answer, Tony swooped her up and carried her to the bedroom.

Walking with ease, Tony negotiated a coffee table, the sofa and the door frame leading into Melinda's bedroom. Swept away with Tony's chivalry, Melinda smiled and admired his bulging biceps flex as he carried her.

Placing Melinda gently onto the bed, Tony positioned himself over her and kissed her mouth softly. He started to divert towards her abdomen, Melinda placed a hand either side of his head and gently pulled it away from her.

Pausing as if he had done something wrong, Melinda broke the awkwardness and softly spoke,

"I want to pleasure you first."

Although Tony liked the sound of this, he could not help remind himself that he had not been with a woman for a long time and feared his pleasure would be over in seconds. Moving off Melinda, Tony rolled onto his back and simultaneously eased off his shoes. Melinda stood back slightly from the bed and unzipped her figure hugging skirt. Tony shuffled uncomfortably, his home made leather cases holding his throwing stars began to dig into his back.

Unsure what Melinda's reaction to these vampire slaying weapons would be Tony decided to take his own jeans off. Arching his back to allow the cases strapped to his belt pass underneath him, he dropped his jeans onto the floor beside the bed. With a hefty thud and a clank the jeans settled in a collapsed pile.

"What you got in there, a V8 engine or something?" Melinda joked,

"Yeah, something, now where were we?"

Melinda started to remove her hold ups,

"Whoa, whoa, if you don't mind leaving them on? You have such fantastic legs they really do compliment them."

"Ok, you're the boss." Melinda cringed slightly, as she realised she had drifted into her professional manner.

Unfazed by her blunder, Tony looked at Melinda like a love struck teenager and waited in anticipation.

Creeping onto the edge of her bed, Melinda walked her fingers up the inside of Tony's leg. Gradually advancing to his groin area, Melinda cat like, made her way over his legs.

Lowering down, she placed a gentle moist kiss just above his right knee. Placing kisses spaced about five inches apart she made her way towards his groin. Lifting her head and sitting upright she calmly spoke,

"You are shaking!"

"Sorry, its been a really long time, since.."

Before Tony could finish his sentence, Melinda interrupted,

"Hey, don't sweat, layback and enjoy the ride. You are in safe hands."

Tony rested his head back into the pillow and briefly closed his eyes, trying to relax.

Finding himself taking a deep breath and feeling a shot of ecstasy flow up his body, he opened his eyes wide and enjoyed the oral pleasure, from Melinda.

Tony fighting the pleasure to avoid it ending to quickly lost the battle. Ejaculating into Melinda's mouth, he juddered and gripped the bed sheets. Melinda an expert in sexual pleasure continued to mouth his penis. Swallowing his warm sperm, she carried on forcing Tony through his ejaculation stage, bringing his limping penis back to fully hard. Tony squirmed, as he went through a rainbow of pleasant sensations and looked down at Melinda.

"Hey, you're good. Now it's my turn, hop on baby."

Melinda mildly amused with Tony's cowboy approach, obeyed and positioned herself and inserted his penis.

Riding him slowly to start with, she gradually increased the momentum and intensity of her strokes. Tony cupped her breasts with both hands and followed her lead.

Watching Melinda ride him hard, Tony noticed her eyes glimmering changing from human to vampire and then back to human, as she approached climax. Tony had managed to filter out the constant glow surrounding her, but found this a little weird. Reminding him that she was still a predator, he decided to keep his guard up just in case she could not control her feeding instincts.

"Ah, ah, ah, ahhhhh, oh my god, Yesssss!" Melinda cried as she came.

Enjoying the sensation till the very end, she bit her bottom lip and realised her fangs had dropped down in her excitement.

Looking frantically at Tony, her fangs quickly retracted.

"Come here, I think you need a cuddle." Tony spoke in a very soft voice.

Taking a moment to absorb the kindness, Melinda lowered herself and placed her head on Tony's chest.

With an expression of butter wouldn't melt, Melinda stared at Tony and thought,

'Oh god, I think I love him.'

Chapter Twenty Three

Tony woke several hours later, taking his time to calculate his whereabouts and recollect that he had just had amazing sex, he sprung upright. Noticing Melinda was no longer sharing the bed, he struggled to believe she had left the room without him hearing her.

Concerned she might be a bad thing for him, he pondered momentarily. Quickly turning his thoughts to one of a fluffy warm feeling of their relationship and focused on that it meant the world to him.

Slowly getting dressed, Tony heard a key entering the front door and then the sound of it opening and quietly closing.

"Hi honnez, I'm home!" Melinda shouted, throwing her keys on a kitchen worktop.

Entering the bedroom, Melinda looked at Tony she was full of the joys of spring and asked,

"And where do you think you are going?"

"Er, I thought you had left, I was just about to see if you had left a note or something."

"Sorry I had to pop out for a bite! Now get those clothes off I'm not done with you yet!"

Tony let out a little laugh and looked at Melinda, realising she had more than one addiction.

"Oh lord what did I do to deserve you?"

Spending a night of serious love making, Tony woke early that morning. Needing to replenish his fluids and fuel his body back to strength, knowing the cupboards to be bare and wondered where might be open. Lying with Melinda neatly tucked into him, he wondered if he could move her leg off him, slip out from her arm and make it to the toilet without waking her.

Looking from the bedroom doorway, Tony admired Melinda's beauty whilst she slept. He weighed up his options, should he leave and remember their time together fondly or should he creep back into bed and be there for when she woke. The more he pondered, the more he convinced himself of the latter.

Tony a competitive man, thought,

'If I cannot get back into bed without waking her, what sort of a Ninja am I?'

Making a route to his side of the bed, in an awfully complicated cat like style, Tony lifted the bed sheets and nestled back into position.

Truly dedicated to his cause, Tony lay still for another hour and a half almost motionless so not to unnaturally wake Melinda.

Feeling her stir, Tony awaited their first real courting morning conversation.

Tony waited, waited and waited some more until finally Melinda awoke.

Stretching her perfectly formed body from tip to toe, Melinda turned and looked at Tony.

"Morning stud muffin."

Although he had waited a long time, the delivery and content was certainly worth waiting for.

"Morning sleepy head." Tony quietly replied,

'Sleepy head, you have been waiting for almost two hours and that is the best you can come up with, you numbskull.' Tony thought.

Tony's stomach grumbled loudly acting as a snooze alarm for Melinda.

"You hungry babes?"

"Yes, my belly thinks my throat has been cut." Realising this might not be the best statement to express in front of a vampire, Tony apologised.

"Sorry, honez you know what I meant."

"Tony, we have our differences but it feels like I should have always known you. Go and feed your belly and hurry back. We need to have our first morning sex."

Chapter Twenty Four

Lifting his head from a young man's neck, the Count injected his serum into the man's blood stream. Taking him by his shoulders the Count positioned him up against a wall and supported him. The man, faint, drifting in and out of consciousness looked at the monster pinning him in position.

"Christian, you will serve me and obey me without question. In return I will provide you with feeding material and a life of riches. Defy me and I will not hesitate in taking your life. You are now man's natural predator and will feed on nothing accept man. Do you understand?"

Christian closed his eyes and murmured,

"Whatever, man."

Releasing his grip on Christian, allowing him to naturally fall forward, the Count dipped down to break his fall. Picking him up in a fireman's type lift, the Count rolled his fingers and teleported to his New York apartment.

Man's Natural Predator

Materialising in his apartment, the Count laid Christian down on his sofa. Looking intensively at Christian, the Count thought,

'I hope you do not follow the path of other guardians, I regretted killing Lee Wong in China. I shouldn't have left Tony without killing him. I should have turned him instead of making him an immortal human, he could become very dangerous. I will not make that mistake again, I sense I have not seen the last of Tony.'

Over the next few weeks Tony and Melinda conducted and appeared as any normal couple in love, to the outside world. Tony had managed to avoid any slaying encounters in an attempt to keep a low profile and protect his identity.

Sitting at a table of a delightful Italian restaurant in Camberley, Tony did not think it strange that Melinda had been spending all her time with him, almost living with him. She had not been back to her flat for over two weeks, only separated when she had to 'pop out' to feed.

Tony fidgeted with his fork, plucking up the courage to ask,

"Why don't you sell your flat and move in with me. You can use the money from the sale to give you your independence. You can feed off me daily; I will be able to repair and survive the blood loss, providing you are not too greedy. What do you say?"

Sitting back in his seat, pleased with the delivery of his pitch, Tony watched Melinda intensely.

Taking a short time before answering, Melinda looked at Tony with pure affection and leant forward clasping his hands.

"Wow, you would do that for me. You could go get any pretty girl, who does not have the baggage."

"Darling, I love you. I wish to spend my life with you, yeah you have baggage but so do I. It feels right. I am willing to go the distance, are you?"

Moving her hands from Tony's she placed them wide on the table. Lifting from her seat she stood and leant as far forward as she could over the table, placing a warm soft kiss on Tony's lips.

Returning to her seat love struck by Tony's gesture, she softly spoke,

"I love you, with all my heart. I know it is early days in our relationship but as you say it feels so right. I would be honoured to spend the rest of my days by your side."

Smiling, Tony pondered if the timing was right to explain a decision that he had recently made. Not wishing to spoil the moment he took a sip of his drink. Returning to his conscience, he felt it only fair that Melinda understood all she was committing to.

"You mentioned you have baggage, well so you understand exactly what you are signing up for, I also have baggage so to speak."

"What, are you talking about Tony?" Melinda interrupted.

"Darling please listen, this is serious. I have taken a long time to come to this decision. I don't know if I have ever told you but the vampire race is all my fault. I released Roberto and brought him back to strength. I understand if you hate me for this but I intend to correct my errors. I will find a cure for you. I will not rest until I have found a way of turning your insides back to human.

I am also going to take on the responsibility of eradicating the rest of the vampire race."

Tony sat nervously, realising he was skating on thin ice, risking his entire relationship with Melinda. Looking at his beloved he licked his lips in an attempt to summon up some saliva to his bone dry mouth.

Taking a reasonable time to contemplate what Tony had just said. Melinda sat back in her seat and folded her arms,

"I suppose this mass eradication involves me as well?"

"No Darling, the way I look at it is if you are feeding from me you are not harming people. Roberto said I was the chosen one and to be honest I did not believe him or think anymore about it. I have a path to follow and the gift to succeed in this quest."

Looking affectionately into Tony's eyes, Melinda also understood why he was the chosen one.

"Let's do it, my sweet." Melinda confirmed.

Moving their hands to the centre of the table they caressed each others hands and looked fondly into each others eyes,

"I propose a toast, to our love, may it be stronger than the demons that are within and around us."

"To us!" Melinda added.

Still looking at each other starry eyed, the silence cemented their bond and eternal love for each other.

Almost perfect timing the waiter brought over Tony's pizza and placed it in front of him.

"Madame, are you sure I can not interest you with anything from the menu?"

"No thank you, I am really not hungry."

Taking a large bite of his pizza, Tony munched away happily. Swallowing his mouthful he looked at Melinda and joked,

"What colour costume should I get? I'm going to also need a utility belt!"

Melinda shook her head briefly and quietly laughed, knowing he was in fact deadly serious.

For a signed copy of my next exciting novel
'The Exterminator'
Email me direct: philbriggs@pjbooks.co.uk

About the Author

For many years, Phil J Briggs devoted his Entreprenual and creative mind to Sales & Marketing. Not fully fulfilled, he decided to jot down his ideas for storylines. Confident he had sufficient material, he wrote his first manuscript, which was soon published as his first book 'Man's Natural Predator.'

'Man's Natural Predator' is the debut novel from Phil J Briggs. The first of many titles, all of which have storylines that will keep you guessing and gripped right until the very last page. Written and designed with both genders in mind, Phil J Briggs has split the boundaries of typical genres, a must read for all.

Printed in the United Kingdom by
Lightning Source UK Ltd., Milton Keynes
140860UK00001B/4/P